The Bending Branch is a work of fiction written by Dianne J. Beale. Any similarities to actual persons, either living or dead, are merely coincidental. All content is the product of the author's imagination and is not to be mistaken, or perceived, as real.

© Copyright 2011 by Dianne J. Beale. All rights reserved. No part of this book may be reproduced, except for brief quotations in articles or reviews, without written permission from the author.

The Bending Branch

The Bending Branch

Chapter 1

Taree *(tah-ree-EH)* hardly noticed the sound of the water as it traveled through the pipes behind her; it had become a natural part of her early routine, bringing a musical rhythm into her essence as she sat curled against the wall under the golden piano. Here she could soak in the calmness around her and gather the strength to again venture out into the elementary school's world that had defied her existence.

By age three, Taree had learned to accommodate those around her. She now easily displayed a proficiency in working near others without becoming a nuisance. Her eyes had long since lost the

The Bending Branch

glow of curiosity and interest; she studied and learned only to avoid the punishments of allowing her grades to drop below perfection. The best answers were the ones that required little thought—just listen to the opinions and facts, mindlessly accepting them, and reiterate them onto the paper. She knew little else was required of her: just change the wording enough so that the sentences would relay the answers while seeming to be her own expressions.

The teachers loved her. She had become a model student. Often they would make the mistake of comparing the other children to her, asking each child why he or she could not be more like her. This, of course, resulted in bullying on the playground and a

The Bending Branch

profound shyness that left Taree friendless and afraid.

And this solitude had no reprieve. At home she was little more than an inconvenience. Expectations ruled here, as well: she followed a strict, predefined regimen. This schedule could only be varied if education demanded it. Otherwise, she knew what she had to do.

Today would begin the fifth grade. Apprehension gripped her as she recalled her parents' warning: two teachers would share her this year to prepare her for the middle school's practice of subject teachers rather than the general practitioner style that had so far applied. One class would be taught by a second teacher who would hold that class in his or her room. The classes

The Bending Branch

would walk quietly down the hall, exchanging teachers, just as if they were heading out for recess or walking to the cafeteria for lunch.

Taree peeled herself off from the wall and crawled out from under her shelter. It was time to eat her breakfast, pack her lunch, grab her backpack, and then head down the path that would lead her to school. As she stood, she unconsciously shook herself: in silence, the well-trained horse seemed to rebel against the rider. Instead, with resolve, she headed down the stairs to begin her day.

Chapter 2

The walk to school proved to be surprisingly uneventful. It seemed that, even with the new protocol, parents or guardians were driving their children to school on this first day.

For a moment, Taree allowed a deep sorrow to rise within her. For as long as she could remember, she had carried the smile of a mysterious woman within her memories. She did not know this person, so far as she knew. Yet the smile carried a warmth and security that Taree longed to feel. She thought of her parents, dignified and relentless, and the smile once again vanished from her mind. Steeling herself, she entered the

The Bending Branch

classroom that was now to be referred to as a homeroom.

As she headed toward the desks, she realized that the surfaces no longer held evidence that they had been assigned. Prior to this year the teachers had seated the students, alphabetically. Since she appeared to be the first student to arrive, she quietly approached the teacher's desk.

"Excuse me, Sir," she managed. Previously her teachers had always been women; this difference made her nervous. Mr. Doyle raised his eyes.

"Oh, hello there, I didn't hear you come in," he acknowledged. "How can I help you?"

Taree took out the class schedule that she had received in the mail. She quietly

The Bending Branch

presented the paper as she continued to talk: "Hi," she responded, cautiously. "I'm Taree Schulz. Is there a particular seat that I should sit in?"

The teacher smiled. "I thought—so long as the class maintains good behavior—that I would allow you students to choose where you would like to sit," he explained.

Taree thanked him, uneasily. Then, remembering a study skills tactic that she had somewhere picked up, she moved to a desk in the front left of the classroom: *Sit in the front left of the classroom. Here you will have fewer distractions. Also, since the professor writes from left to right, you will be the first to see the notes that he is writing.*

The Bending Branch

Because she was lost in thought, she failed to notice that her teacher had continued talking. A dark red spread across her face as another student, who had just entered the room, answered the teacher's question. "I'm sorry, Sir," she stammered. "I didn't realize that you were still talking to me."

The teacher's smile never left his face. "That's okay, Taree. The fifth grade is a new experience for all of you. I am sure that you'll do better during class time."

Taree wanted to sink into the floor. Instead she thanked him and quietly began to set up her desk for the day. The other student, Matthew, plopped down in front of her. Turning, he grimaced, "I'm going to show you up this year." She decided to ignore him.

The Bending Branch

Matthew got good grades despite his unruliness in class. For a moment, she contemplated changing seats . . . he had pulled her hair all throughout the first grade when he had been seated behind her. She had consistently put up with his antics. But, with the teacher outside the classroom, Taree had finally raised herself from her seat, turned around, and shoved him. The classroom had exploded in a round of applause as Matthew had flown across the empty desks and seats behind him. He had then threatened to beat her up after school. She remembered how he had run to his bus that very afternoon. The teacher had defended Taree's actions, smugly telling Matthew that obviously Taree had had a

The Bending Branch

good reason for doing what she did since *she* was the better student.

Presently, Taree frowned. She was not proud of her past behavior. She quietly responded, "I hope you do."

Matthew looked at a loss for words. The teacher continued smiling.

Chapter 3

The day had dragged by. If Taree had wanted to change her seating arrangements, she would have had to have done so prior to signing the seating chart that the teacher had passed around. It appeared to be of no consequence, though. Matthew had been the model student throughout the entire day. Surprisingly, he seemed to have his act together this year, even more so than Taree. Involuntarily, she shrugged.

"Hey, Taree!" called a winded classmate. "Wait up! We can walk together."

Samantha had not spoken to Taree since they had shared a teacher in

The Bending Branch

Kindergarten. Still, so as not to ruffle adult feathers, Taree slowed her pace. When Samantha arrived at her side, she forced, "Hi Samantha," to move out from her lips.

True to her form, Samantha began to prattle. She talked of how cute Matt had become over the summer and of how lucky Taree was to be sitting near to him. She spoke of her parents and how they told her she would be walking to school this year *to show responsibility*. She insisted that she and Taree would, of course, be walking together. And she enveloped Taree into a hurried hug just before racing off to the neighboring house.

The rest of the week, and following months, moved along in the same way.

The Bending Branch

But then, Taree received her first grade below an A.

On this particular day, having learned from past experience that it was best to get unpleasant things over with as quickly as possible, she had placed the offending schoolwork onto the kitchen table and disappeared under her trusted, golden piano. Then she waited. The tears flowed rhythmically with the sound of the water as it ran through the pipes.

But she was silent in her distress, burying her tears into her shirt as she had so often done before. Words from her mother (although soft-spoken) echoed within her mind: *No daughter of mine is going to use the excuse that she is a girl, to cry. Tears do nothing. Just get it right next time.*

The Bending Branch

Taree instinctively wiped her nose and face, slid out from beneath the piano, and moved into the bathroom to wash off the evidence of her tears. She was putting in eye drops just as she heard her mother call from below.

"Taree, have you spoken to your teacher about this grade? Taree? Where are you, girl? I want to talk to you . . . Now!"

Just as her mom had finished, Taree had taken her appropriate, nearby stance. "I couldn't talk to the teacher yet," she stammered. "He had a teacher's meeting today after school and told me to come in early for school on Monday."

"I see," her mother quipped. "Take this upstairs, then. I don't want your father to see it until you have spoken to your teacher."

Although her mother was usually the parent to hide from, Taree knew that grades were the one thing that her father would also obsess over. She would have preferred to just get this over with and could not help but feel that her mother was intentionally making this worse for her.

"Yes, mother," she answered. "I'm sorry to have bothered you with it."

Inside, Taree felt as if she were drowning. She had never been given a grade lower than an A. Had her frivolous response to Matt been prophetic? Had she given fate the idea that Matt should be the one to succeed? Did fate think she no longer deserved to be at the top

The Bending Branch

because of her thoughtless response on that first day?

Taree took the paper and ran up the stairs to her room. She placed it into her book, inside her backpack, and slid back under her golden piano. She did not hear the phone ring.

At dinner, since it was Friday, the whole family sat at the table. Her mother let her know that she had been invited to Samantha's for a sleepover and that it was already decided that this was how her Saturday night would be spent.

Despite not wanting to attend, Taree just accepted the news and remained quietly at the table until all had finished their food. Her parents then rushed off to their life demands while Taree cleaned up. The phone, again, rang.

The Bending Branch

"Hello?"

"Hi, Taree, it's Matt. Can you talk? Is this a good time to call?"

He didn't seem nervous at all. "Yes, I have time to talk," she stammered.

"I wanted to warn you about Samantha's party. I don't know what they're planning, but I did hear them saying that it would be a night that you would never forget. It didn't sound like a good thing, either. You should find a way to not go. Just saying."

Taree thanked him and then asked if he knew of a way that she could make herself sick. He laughed at her naïveté and gave her a list of possibilities. Then he told her not to tell anyone that he had called and he hung up.

The Bending Branch

Chapter 4

Taree purposely put her paper back out on the table despite knowing that her mother would be furious. This seemed the surest way to avoid Samantha's stupid sleepover. Then she headed off to bed.

In the morning, Taree's dad quietly lectured her about her B+ grade and told her that she was grounded for the rest of the school year. "This means that you are not going to Samantha's," he added.

Her mother just scowled at her. Despite knowing that she had, once again, disappointed them both, this was the first time that she recalled feeling as if she were dancing inside her head. She apologized, profusely, said she would talk to the teacher, and then excused herself to her room without delay. There, she threw herself onto the bed and laughed into the pillows in triumph.

As was the custom, Taree went without food for the rest of the day. She knew that, this time, her father would not be sneaking her food behind her mother's back. But Taree was relieved that her social life would not be a problem for the rest of the school year.

Monday came, too soon, but at least the ritual of Samantha and she walking together had stopped. It did not occur to Taree how odd it seemed that no one had been taunting her on her way to, and from, school as she had grown accustomed. She was moving stuff

The Bending Branch

around in her locker when she realized why.

    Thomas had deliberately shoved her by feigning that he had tripped while passing by. He then had taken her bagged lunch and had thrown it into the nearby trash bin, commenting that it was not even fit to feed to the dog that she was. Matt had instantly told Thomas to leave her alone—that she was a good kid. Everything had suddenly become clear.

    The conversation with the teacher had not gone so well, though. The B+ was a higher grade than he had wanted to give. He told her that his writing class required creativity and imagination. Although her grammar, penmanship, and answers were flawless, he could not give her the grade of an A if she was not

The Bending Branch

willing to express her own thoughts and ideas. He did not want her to regurgitate what he had said. He wanted her to think for herself—to provoke thoughtful discussion. This was something that Taree had never been taught to do.

By the end of fifth grade, Taree felt defeated. She had a report card that was filled with grades of A and even A+. But in her writing class, the class for which she did not have Mr. Doyle, she had consistently received grades of B to B+. Her parents ignored her A and A+ grades to instead concentrate on the one B+ grade; they were now discussing sending her off to a boarding school. The mysterious, smiling woman disappeared from her memories.

The Bending Branch

Chapter 5

An all-girls' boarding school may have been intolerable had it not been for the letters that she had received from Matthew. Her parents had finally decided that she would attend the local middle school. Directly after the sixth grade, however, she was shipped off to relatives in Germany. Her name, *tah-ree-EH,* had consistently been changed to t*er- ree.* She learned to hate this name.

The one thing that boarding school had saved her from, though, was the continued, ridiculous bias that the sixth grade teachers had shown toward Matthew. Although inexcusable, this had continued throughout the rest of his pre-

The Bending Branch

college education. In fact, Matthew had become so dispirited that he had stopped trying. He had allowed his grades to fall and had decided not to attend a university. But his letters to Taree had never revealed any of this. They provided her with many hours of relaxed laughter and enjoyment.

It did not seem to matter that Matthew Sager had held good grades all through the elementary school, despite his antics, or that, in the fifth grade, he had significantly matured and had shed his previous, class clown stigma. Once he had moved into middle school and beyond, the teachers judged him according to the reputation of his older siblings: "Not another *Sager*," they would say. But Taree was spared from seeing or

The Bending Branch

hearing of his persecution and a strong friendship had formed.

Two months into college, Taree received her final letter from Matt. It had come inside a package from his parents, so she knew that the news would not be good. He had written a letter that had never been mailed out and that actually said to only mail it if he had not made it home from his travels. His parents wrote a really nice letter to go along with the one that he had wished for her to have; it mostly thanked her for being such a good friend and for believing in him when others had not.

Taree's parents never knew the pain that she suffered after receiving this letter. They did not know that she had flown to be with his parents at the

The Bending Branch

funeral. They did not ask what the money was for and she did not tell them.

They were never aware that she was getting straight-A grades while seeing a weekly counselor. They also did not realize that, in her mind, they had been replaced as parents . . . they were nothing more than monetary guardians while Matt's parents had become her solace and support.

And only she knew that her valedictorian speech had derived from Matt's final letter to her. Among the many words, he had written: *Your name, Taree, is of Japanese origin. It means bending branch. You are strong, Taree. Many times you have been forced to bend much farther than a person probably should, but you bend without breaking.*

The Bending Branch

You are an inspiration to those who truly know you. Thank you for bending toward me . . . for being such a great friend. Remember the smiling woman.

He had included a picture that he had drawn: a beautiful, smiling woman. It was based on a description that she had given him some time during the beginning of the fifth grade, directly after she had received her first below-A grade.

No one knew that Matt was the reason that she was able to stay above water in that one class. Without him, she would not have even achieved the B grades that she had received. He was also the grounds for why she was happy with her achievements, despite the lower grades.

The Bending Branch

Chapter 6

"Taree, do you know where we put your grandparents' presents? We should be loading them into the car already. Did your dad take them out to the car with him? You did remember to buy them gifts of your own, right? We don't put your name on our gifts anymore."

Taree had finished college and now lived in an apartment of her own. She had arrived at her parents' the night before and they were leaving to her grandparents' today. It was obvious that they were driving out to her father's parents' this Christmas. This had always made her mother nervous, turning her usual silence in to edgy conversation.

The Bending Branch

"Yes, Mom, I have my own gifts for Gramm and Gramp. I don't know about yours. Want me to go check?"

"Would you mind? I still need to pack the food we're taking."

"I'm going outside now. Don't talk to me while I'm gone, okay?"

"Very funny. Just go out and ask your dad."

Her mother would do this, though. She would talk while you were out of the room and then expect whoever she thought she'd been talking to to have answers or to have done something. Taree repeated herself. "I'm already halfway out the door. Stop talking now because I won't be able to hear you."

The Bending Branch

Her father, overhearing, chided her: "Don't tease your mother, Taree. Why aren't you making yourself useful?"

Taree ignored her father's jabs. "Mom wants to know if you packed the presents yet. "

"I thought *she* was in charge of the presents. She wants me to do *that*, too?"

Her dad sounded annoyed. "I'll go tell her, *no*, then." She left without giving her dad time to reply. She hated being in the middle.

By the time they were packed and ready to go, Taree was regretting that she had not opted to drive straight to her grandparents'. The drive would have been long without this convenient stopping point, but the tension between her parents was reminding her of the

The Bending Branch

time when Samantha had dragged her down under the water and then pulled her along until her lungs had felt as if they would pop if she did not open her mouth. Luckily, the life guard had seen and had come to the rescue just in time to prevent Taree from breathing water in through her mouth.

Relief only came when they stopped at a restaurant for lunch. Her parents transformed again into adults and were behaving in the stifling, dignified manner that she had grown accustomed to when she had lived at home.

The remainder of the car ride was accomplished in silence with only slight interruptions for requested bathroom breaks. Taree began to wonder if maybe the fight that she had avoided by leaving her car in her parents' garage might have been the better option.

The visit went only downhill from here. The first comment to come out of her grandmother's mouth was that her granddaughter should be married with children by now. Her grandmother had an artistic knack for complimenting people only to cut them down at the same time: "You are such an intelligent and beautiful young lady. Why are you not yet married? Will I get to see my great-grandchildren before I die? What is the matter with you that you don't yet have a rich and handsome husband?"

This had immediately caused her mom to bristle. Although Taree's mom actually had a better job than her father, his parents refused to acknowledge this.

The Bending Branch

Grandma had often complained how her son had married beneath himself.

Taree's dad did nothing to ease the situation. He did not defend his daughter and he chose to ignore his wife. Sometimes he interacted with his mother as if he were still a child living under the same roof.

Grandpa, as usual, just remained distant, standing to the side as if not related in any way. Soon they had all gone inside, each carrying two or more bundles; although awkward, there would be no need to return to the car.

Chapter 7

Later, Taree phoned Matt's parents. They had a running joke that if she needed to look as if she were dating someone then she could just go off to where she could be seen, but not heard, and call them from her phone. Everyone would then think that she was dating a nice, young man. She explained that this is what she was doing at the moment although it was a breath of fresh air to talk with them, as well. They just laughed, told her that they missed her, and then released her to return to her family. They were kind to speak with her since the noise in the background

The Bending Branch

suggested that they had more than a full house.

After Christmas, Taree returned to her quiet, small apartment. As she was unlocking her door, she noticed that a new neighbor had moved in across the hall.

She had hoped to avoid socializing. Since their eyes had met, however, she felt obligated to voice a greeting. She threw a hello over her shoulder and then carried her bag into the apartment. As she returned to the door to go back out for the rest of her belongings from the car, a tall, muscular shape was framed inside the neighboring door.

He held out his hand. "Hi, I'm Rinji *(rin-jee).*"

The Bending Branch

Taking his outstretched hand, she replied, "Taree. Nice to meet you."

As soon as the introductions were done, Rinji moved back inside his apartment. Although he left his door open, Taree closed hers. Rinji did not appear to be a threat, but still she was silently thankful that it had an automatic lock. She used the elevator to head back downstairs. After two more trips, she had finished unloading her car and had retreated to her apartment.

The Bending Branch

Chapter 8

Rinji sat in his apartment, feeling perplexed. "Why did this woman possess a Japanese name?" he wondered. He began to think that maybe his parents had somehow managed to interfere, once more, with his life. He picked up the phone only to place it, again, onto its charger.

Just as he decided to cross over to close his door, Taree opened hers. "We've got to stop meeting like this," she joked. She was on her way to the lobby to pick up her mail. Rinji merely nodded at her and then closed his door while she moved toward the elevator.

The Bending Branch

"He barely acknowledged me," she thought to herself. "Well, it's not like I was trying to get his attention, right?" She began to shuffle through her mail as she waited for the elevator's return.

"It's stuck again," she heard from across the way. She looked up to see one of the two residents of the remaining apartment on her floor. Angie was a bodacious blonde with brilliant white teeth, smooth, Latin skin, and skin-tight dance outfits. She was also married to an equally stunning woman by the name of Cherise.

"Oh, hi Angie. Really? But I just rode it down not five minutes ago."

"Yeah, well . . . Little Ms. Perfection is holding it on her floor again."

The Bending Branch

"I thought she was told not to do that anymore."

"She was."

"Oh. Well, thanks. I guess I'll take the stairs then."

"You do that, Honey." Angie headed out to the street and Taree opened the door to use the stairs. As she exited the stairwell, she that noticed Rinji was also waiting for the elevator.

"Angie—she's from that apartment over there—just told me that the lady on the next floor down is holding the elevator again. You might want to take the stairs," she offered.

"Does that happen often?" Rinji queried, without even looking up.

"Often enough for us to have filed multiple complaints. She's not supposed

The Bending Branch

to do it, but I don't think she really cares. She's dating the manager's son so thinks she has special privileges. Angie calls her Little Ms. Perfection. They can't stand each other. I just try to kind of stay out of the way."

"I see. I guess I'll take the stairs then."

Taree disappeared into her apartment. She had the distinct feeling that she had somehow offended this new neighbor. But what could she have done differently? Wouldn't it have been worse if she'd ignored him? "I hate social stuff," she sighed. "I miss Matt. He was so good at those things."

The Bending Branch

Chapter 9

Awaking with a throbbing body and an exceptionally sore throat, Taree struggled to remember the day. Was it Monday? Friday? She couldn't seem to remember. Climbing out from bed, she crossed the room to the dresser and picked up her phone. It was Sunday. Thank goodness.

Putting on a kettle of water, she took down her shelf organizer that contained all of the medicine. Taking out a packet of powdered flu medicine, she returned the box to the shelf.

After drinking the warm medicine, Taree took a hot shower and then climbed back into bed. Four hours later,

The Bending Branch

she was awake and aching again. This time she remembered having seen a large bruise on her side when she had showered. Lifting her shirt, she suddenly had the recollection of the close quarters within her grandparents' hallways. She had collided with her dad when he had opened the door to the bedroom where he and her mother had stayed. Relieved to see it was only a bruise, she then decided that maybe she should get it checked. She picked up the phone to call Matt's mother, a nurse, to ask if this was really a necessary step. She was happy that Mom Sager thought that it could wait.

When the doorbell rang, Taree didn't think twice about answering it. She mainly practiced sleeping in large, warm, sweat suits during the winter. It was Cherise.

"Hi, Cherise. Did you need something?"

Cherise tried to smile. "Have you seen Angie today?" she asked.

"Not since I got the mail when I arrived home last night. Why, is something wrong?"

Cherise seemed to wane a bit. "I'm not sure," she puzzled. "I thought I heard her come in last night but I don't recall actually seeing her. This morning she's just not here. There's no note or anything."

"Do you have her dance schedule?" Taree offered. "Maybe she's in another production or something."

The Bending Branch

"She always hangs one on the fridge. But that seems to be missing, as well."

Taree grabbed her keys from the nearby key tree and moved out into the hall. "There should be another on the bulletin board downstairs." Cherise followed as Taree headed down the staircase.

The schedule showed that Angie did have a show to perform both that morning and the night before. Cherise apologized for her flightiness, thanked Taree and then headed out to her car. She promised to let her know if there was a problem. Taree nodded as she went back through the door, up the stairs, and into her apartment.

The Bending Branch

The doorbell rang once more. This time it was Rinji. "Are you okay?" he asked.

"Yes. Why?"

"Last night there was some kind of fight in the hallway. By the time I was awake enough to fully realize it, the noise had died down and the hallway was empty."

"You opened your door when you thought you'd heard a fight? Don't you think that might have been a bit dangerous? I usually just call the police."

"Well, I guess I wasn't too worried. The crime here is supposed to be much lower than what I've been used to," Rinji explained.

"I hope Angie's okay. Her roommate, Cherise, was just here asking me about

The Bending Branch

her. I believe she has an ex who sometimes drinks too much and becomes abusive. I didn't hear a thing: not last night or this morning."

"Well, I tend to be a light sleeper."

Taree shrugged. "I suppose I may have just grown accustomed to it. It hasn't happened in over a year, though. I think I'll call the dance studio, just to check on her. I'll have to go back to the lobby to get the number."

"I thought you said that you prefer to just kind of stay out of the way," Rinji mused.

"Well, that is usually the best policy . . ." Taree's voice trailed off.

Rinji chuckled. "I'll come with you. Just in case."

The Bending Branch

The dance studio placed Angie on the phone almost immediately. Her ex had followed her home the night before, as Taree had suspected, but he was too drunk to be of any real threat. Angie had called the police and then had to file a report at the station. So, all was well, for the most part. Angie and Cherise were finally filling out a restraining order.

"Thanks, Rinji," Taree said as they rode the elevator back up to their floor. "I hope that things quiet down. I'm sorry that this happened so soon after you moved in."

"Why are you apologizing? I'm not sure I follow." Again, he laughed.

"I tend to do that," admitted Taree. "Matt would be disappointed."

The Bending Branch

As soon as the words left her mouth, she regretted them. Rinji did not know who Matt was and she had basically just closed a door in his face. Maybe he wouldn't notice.

"So, this fellow Matt, do you spend a lot of time with him?" he prompted.

"Not so much," Taree blushed.

"Why not?"

"He decided to travel after high school. I think he may have even joined the army. I've never really been told the whole story, but he died. I still have fond thoughts of him, though."

"I'm sorry. I shouldn't have . . ."

"Now who's apologizing without reason? I'm the one who brought him up."

The Bending Branch

"Right. Well I've got to get moving. Have a good day."

"You, too. Thanks for checking on me."

"No problem."

Taree watched him as he unlocked and then entered his apartment. She had scared him off.

The Bending Branch

Chapter 10

Years later, Rinji and Taree had remained friends. Neither lived anywhere near the apartment building in which they had met, but they still lived in the same town. They tried to visit whenever they could and each did his or her best to remember to call on holidays and birthdays.

On her twenty-sixth birthday, after her parents had downsized their house, she inherited the golden piano. She invited Rinji over to hear her play.

Rinji was in awe of how good the piano sounded despite its obvious need of a tuning. He soon was inspecting it and asking many questions. Taree could

The Bending Branch

answer very few: she knew so little about the piano that she had inherited.

Rinji copied numbers and words from off the piano. The brand had been painted over, but he was convinced that the piano was a Steinway.

Taree was amused by his enthusiasm and assured him that this was most likely to be as far from the truth as could possibly be. Why would someone paint a Steinway?

But Rinji still copied everything he could find from the panels that did not bear the golden paint. "Why *is* the piano gold?" he asked.

"It's been that color my whole life," she answered. "I realize that someone must have painted it, since the brand

The Bending Branch

name doesn't show up anywhere, but it's been gold for as long as I can remember."

"I see. And is this the piano that you learned to play?"

"We had two pianos. This piano was in my bedroom. I practiced on it and had lessons on the one downstairs."

"So your parents still have a piano," he remarked, casually.

"I would guess so, unless they sold it with their house."

"What is the brand of their piano? Are they both grands?"

Taree blushed. "We had a very large house, especially for a family of three. They were both grand pianos, but the one downstairs was a Bosendorfer. It was my dad's piano when he was growing up. It's magnificent! I think it is made of mahogany and walnut. I'm not sure where we got my golden piano. I just know I've always had it."

"So your dad plays, too?"

"And my mom. My dad, along with most of my instructors, wanted me to become a concert pianist. No one realizes I only play well because I play when I am sad. Music brings me out from my sadness. And I'm not sad so much anymore."

Rinji decided to tease her. "So when did this sadness begin to recede? About the time you met me, maybe?" When she threw him her strongest oh-please look, he began to chuckle.

Taree decided to gradually change the subject. "Why are you so interested in pianos? How come you seem to know so much? Did you study music, too?"

Rinji shook his head. "My dad worked with Yamaha for a time. The only formal music education that I ever had ended in the grade schools, I think. You know—the required school classes."

"I hated those."

"Me, too."

"So how come you think this is a Steinway?"

"When my dad worked for Yamaha, I went with him to music stores quite a bit. He and I would discuss the differences of the pianos on the floor. I got pretty good at recognizing which brands were which, even from a distance."

"Ah, I see." Taree glanced over at Rinji. He said *I see* rather often. She wondered

The Bending Branch

if he'd catch that she was trying to copy him.

He did. "You need more practice," is all he said.

The Bending Branch

Chapter 11

As they ate the food that they had delivered, it grew silent. Rinji sensed that he was here for moral support but wasn't sure why. Did the piano, itself, cause her sadness? If it did, maybe cleaning it up and proving it was a Steinway would allow her to sell it, along with the heaviness that he was sensing.

Taree finally spoke up. "Rinji?"

"Yes?"

"Can I tell you about Matt?"

"If you'd like," Rinji agreed. She had rarely mentioned Matt since the day he'd knocked on her door and had asked if she was okay.

The Bending Branch

"When he and I were in grade school—the first grade, I think—he sat behind me. He would twist my braid around his finger during class and then yank my hair at least once or twice per day. Since he was already always getting into trouble, I did my best to ignore it. I was shy then and often the teachers would tell the other kids that if I could get the grades they were looking for then there was no excuse for their lesser grades. But Matt had the same grades I did; he just behaved like the class clown so that this would go unnoticed. I had very few friends and was often bullied."

Taree paused, but only for a moment. "One day, when the teacher went out into the hall to speak to the principal, Matt pulled my hair extra hard. I don't know

The Bending Branch

why, but I stood up and turned around to confront him. He quickly stood, as well. I shoved him really hard and he flew over a couple of chairs and desks and then fell to the floor. The teacher came quickly back into the room and asked what had happened. He told her that I had pushed him and she only said that he probably deserved it. When she went back out into the hall, he whispered that he was going to beat me up that night. I walked, alone, to and from school at the time. I was truly afraid. Then, that afternoon, I saw him nervously scanning for me and then he ran to his bus."

Rinji shifted in his seat. Taree looked up to see if he seemed annoyed. He was listening, waiting for her to go on, so Taree continued. "In the fifth grade, I had

The Bending Branch

my first male teacher. In fact, I had two male teachers because the school had two teachers who teamed up and exchanged their classes for one subject. This was to prepare us for the multiple classrooms and teachers we would have in middle school. My homeroom teacher was just as happy with my work as those I had had previously. He became one of my most favorite teachers—Mr. Doyle. But my English teacher, no matter how hard I tried, never gave me above a B+.

Matt and I became friends that year. He is the reason that I was able to maintain a B to B+ grade in that class. I also discovered that he had been protecting me from the other kids. He surpassed me that year. "

The Bending Branch

Taree sighed, as if the next portion of her story was difficult to tell. "In sixth grade, Matt was on the other side of the school and we no longer shared classes. We had different sixth grade halls and teachers. We rarely saw one another. Then my parents shipped me off to an all-girls' boarding school; that summer I moved to Germany. I didn't even get to say good-bye to him. So, I sent him a letter and we became pen pals. The next time I saw him, though, he was lying in a coffin and his parents were standing next to me, one on each side. His brothers and sisters were lined up on the other side. And now I keep in touch with his parents as best I can."

Rinji was surprised to realize that he was relieved: Taree and Matt had truly

The Bending Branch

been no more than friends. If he had not been sitting across from her, he might have scolded himself. Taree and he were also no more than friends, so why should he feel relieved? Had he considered Matt to be competition? Had he been jealous of their relationship?

When Rinji didn't say anything, Taree looked over to see why. He seemed to be deep in thought. She decided to share something that she had not even shared with Matt.

"The golden piano served as my one, true friend. I played it when I was sad. I sat under it for protection and a sense of security. I talked to it whenever I had problems and I cried into its leg whenever I was so completely miserable that I couldn't find the strength to play.

The Bending Branch

And my parents ripped this friend from my grasp by sending me away to Germany. Matt became my new friend, but I no longer had the depth of friendship that came with my piano. Without Matt's letters, I'm not sure I would have survived the boarding school. I was an outsider, always looking in. And my German relatives did not speak English to me even though they could. So, at first, I was alone."

Taree yawned and then continued. "It's ironic. Now again, I have my golden piano, but I no longer need it; I've learned to live without it. Yet I find it comforting that we will be together again."

She had almost made the mistake of admitting to Rinji that he had become

The Bending Branch

her golden piano. He was the reason that she didn't need it. She was relieved that she had not confessed this. It might have chased him away.

Rinji finally spoke up. "My dad is an expert when it comes to pianos. Would you like me to have him come to look at it? He could probably even remove the gold paint, but only if you'd like. He might be able to restore it . . . return it to its true from."

Taree had never met Rinji's parents. She wasn't sure that this would be a good idea. What if his dad didn't like her?

Her German relatives had a habit of calling her *Schwächling* (*swy –sling*). It had become her name for those many years. At first, before she knew what it meant, it was truly how they had seen

The Bending Branch

her. Later, once she had adapted and had become fluent in German, it had become a term of endearment. *Schwächling* meant weakling. Taree smiled; they had shown her the love that her parents could not. They had made her strong.

Rinji was growing nervous at the silence. Had he been too bold? Had he misunderstood her relationship to the piano? Did she think his offer for his dad to look at the piano meant more than it did? "I'm sorry, Taree," he said, quietly. "I didn't mean to offend you." Rinji didn't get to finish his thought.

Taree interrupted him, "No. You didn't offend me. I do want to know more about my piano. It's just . . ."

"I didn't mean to pry," Rinji softly replied as Taree trailed off.

The Bending Branch

Taree realized that she would have to reveal more than she had planned. She would have to tell him about the mysterious, smiling woman. "You're not prying," she explained. "Another reason that Matt was so important to me is because he reminded me of a memory that I'd forgotten. Up until the end of fifth grade, I carried a remote recollection of a mysterious woman that was smiling down at me. I had told Matt about her."

Taree crossed the room to her desk and took out a box. She walked back over to Rinji. Opening the box, she removed a picture, handing it to him. "I had forgotten about her. Matt drew this after I had told him about her during one of our fifth-grade English assignments. He sent it to me with his final letter and instructed me to remember her. I've always thought that the piano has something to do with her. I guess maybe that is why I blocked her from my mind."

"Did you not play piano while you were in Germany?" Rinji queried.

Taree looked surprised. "I hadn't thought about it, but no, I didn't. Not really. We did sing carols at Christmas time and I accompanied on their untuned upright. But otherwise, no."

"You didn't come home for Christmas?" Rinji was stunned.

"Well, most of the time, no. I think maybe once or twice when Christmas was at my dad's parents' house. Otherwise, I don't think I did. That reminds me, I forgot to call them this

The Bending Branch

Christmas—my relatives in Germany, I mean."

Rinji looked down at the drawing in his hands. "Matt was very talented," he observed. "She's very pretty. Is she Japanese?"

"I always thought that she must be. But I don't know who she is. I don't remember ever meeting her."

"Can I ask you something?"

"Of course," Taree smiled.

"Have you ever met your mother's parents?"

"No, I haven't. I know nothing of them. That subject is taboo in my home. Even with me free to romp around in the house during all the hours when my parents weren't home, I've never found a trace of evidence that they even exist. I know that she has to have had parents, but I've always assumed they must be dead. I've never found photos, letters, or any other evidence that they are alive."

"Could she maybe be your grandmother, then?"

Taree had never thought of this possibility. Would her parents have hidden this from her? Why would they keep her from her grandparents? But to answer Rinji honestly, she confessed: "I hate to say it, but . . . with my parents, anything is possible." She had a frown etched into her face.

Rinji instantly regretted the question. He frowned, too.

"Why do you ask?" Taree inquired. She knew that Rinji had to have a reason.

The Bending Branch

"You have the same color of eyes, even the same expression. I suppose that maybe Matt might have done that, though, unconsciously."

"No. I don't think so. She looks exactly as I remember describing her to him. His picture immediate evoked my lost memory. I remember watching as he drew her. I asked him to keep her so my parents would not find her."

"I see," was all Rinji said.

The Bending Branch

Chapter 12

Today was the day that Taree was meeting with Rinji and his dad. They were to arrive within the next hour.

Taree had spent the day cleaning and polishing her piano as she had been taught by her father. She was just now coming out from the shower.

As she rummaged through her clothes, she was embarrassed to admit that she really wanted Rinji's dad to like her. She knew that Rinji greatly valued his parents' opinions and advice. He had a high regard for their wisdom and instruction and held a very strict moral code.

The Bending Branch

When had she foolishly allowed herself to fall in love with Rinji? She swiftly became aware that she hadn't fallen at all—she had steadily walked along and the love had grown as if a garden beside her path.

When the doorbell rang, she made a quick selection from her wall of clothes, pulled it on, and headed out to answer the door. Instinctively, she had chosen her deep purple pant suit. Her hunches were usually correct.

Upon opening the door, Taree was surprised to find, along with Rinji and his father, Rinji's mother. To ease her anxiety, Rinji quickly explained. "My dad repairs and refinishes pianos, but he needs my mom in order to tune them."

The Bending Branch

Taree recovered, flawlessly. It appeared that Rinji also wanted her to make a good impression. She was relieved. Stepping aside, she invited them in.

On the coffee table she had set out coffee, creamer, sugar, tea, sodas, and appetizers that she had prepared that morning: decorative tea sandwiches with cubes of different types of cheese. She led them into the living room area and offered the food and drinks.

Rinji's parents quietly sat down on the love couch and Rinji took the matching arm chair. Taree sat on the chair that she had moved over from her small kitchen set. As they ate together, she did her best to answer any questions and to provide any information that she could share about the piano. She apologized that she didn't really know more and admitted that her father had not gotten back to her with any updated information.

Finally, they all moved to the piano's side. Rinji's mom spoke up: "Could you play something simple for us?" she requested.

Taree quietly sat at the piano and played one the earliest pieces that she could remember. When she was finished, she rose again and moved back to the piano's side. There were tears in Rinji's father's eyes: "That was beautiful," he simply offered. "It's one of my favorites from when I was a kid." He moved over to take a closer look at the piano.

While Rinji's dad was inspecting the piano, his mom began to make light conversation with Taree. "Your name is Japanese. Do you have Japanese relatives?"

Taree answered as honestly as she could. "Well, I'm not really sure. My father is German. I lived for awhile in Germany, with his relatives, when I was younger. I don't know anything about my mother."

"Oh. Did she die?"

Taree grew nervous. "No, she just doesn't *want* me to know. When I did a family tree in fourth grade, she made me put only my father's history. She sent me to school with a note to the teacher stating that her side was not available."

Rinji's mom persisted. "Is she ashamed of who she is?"

The Bending Branch

"I . . . I don't know for sure." Taree was beginning to think that Rinji was off limits.

The questioning continued. "Does she look Japanese?"

"No, not really," Taree admitted.

And again. "You played a Japanese song. Why's that?"

Taree didn't really have an answer. She began to fear that Rinji's parents thought that she was being elusive on purpose. "It's the first song I learned, I think. I don't even remember learning it. Sometimes it feels as if I was born knowing it." Taree trailed off. She shivered. Once again she had the feeling of being utterly alone in the world. Rinji's parents didn't like her.

The Bending Branch

His dad broke in, "Can I take this piano to my workshop, young woman? I'm pretty sure it's a Steinway but I'd like to remove this gold paint. Can I do that?"

Taree didn't know how to answer. She had believed Rinji's idea to have been a good one. Now she was miserable. She felt the isolation of having only one friend again . . . her golden piano. She could feel Rinji slipping away.

He still came to her rescue. "I think Taree needs time to think about that, Dad. She's had this piano all of her life. I don't think I prepared her for the possibility that the piano would have to be moved. She just got it here last week."

Rinji's mom snorted. "Well she can't have expected us to repair it here. This

The Bending Branch

project could take weeks, maybe months!"

Taree tried again. "I'm sorry. I didn't realize that this would all go so quickly. I thought I'd get an assessment and then an estimate and then I'd make a decision. I guess I must have misunderstood..."

Rinji's mom interrupted. "Never mind then. We'll go now and if you decide to do something then you can let us know." She tugged on her husband's arm. "Let's go, dear," she insisted. She thrust a business card into Taree's hand as she continued walking forward. Taree handed a business card to Rinji's dad.

Rinji walked his parents to the door and then turned. "I'll call you, okay?"

"Okay. Thank you for your time," Taree breathed.

The Bending Branch

Then they were gone. Taree walked back to her piano and sat on the bench. In anguish, she began to play.

The Bending Branch

Chapter 13

After about an hour, Taree cleaned up the apartment and then ran a hot bath. She poured in some jasmine bath beads and then went back out from the bathroom to check her windows and doors. Once she was sure that all was locked, with curtains closed, she went into her bedroom, stripped, and then pulled on her luxurious robe.

She returned to the bathroom, shut the door, put on some jazz, and then climbed into the tub. She closed her eyes and did her best to shut out the rest of the world.

The Bending Branch

When the doorbell rang, Taree was surprised to realize that she was still soaking in a tub where the water had gone cold. She climbed out, dried off, and then pulled on her robe. She went to the door and peered out the peephole. It was Rinji. She left the chain locked and cracked the door. "What are you doing here?" she questioned.

"You weren't answering your phone," he explained. "I thought you were avoiding me."

"Why would I do that?" Taree was still not fully awake and wasn't thinking about the earlier disaster.

"Would you have to have a reason?" he teased. "I thought women were allowed to be unreasonable."

The Bending Branch

"Have I been unreasonable? When? I'm sorry if I've upset you."

"No Taree," he answered. "I was just being silly. Can I come in? The hall's a bit cold tonight."

"I'm not dressed," she admitted. "I was headed off to bed."

"At eight?" he asked, in disbelief.

Taree didn't know what to say. "Okay. I guess you can come in." She undid the chain and opened the door. "Make yourself at home. I'll just go get dressed."

As Taree meandered into the bedroom and shut the door, Rinji made his way over to the piano. He opened the bench. It was empty. He then went to the refrigerator and stacked a plate with the luncheon leftovers. Then he sat down on the couch.

The Bending Branch

Taree returned, shortly, in her customary sweatshirt and pants. Plopping down next to him, she asked if he needed anything to drink.

He laughed. "You sit first and then ask? No, I'm fine, thanks. I'd love to make you get back up but there's really no reason." He pointed to the soda can that sat to the left of his feet. She'd forgotten she'd gotten canned sodas for the luncheon.

Taree sank further into the love seat. "So, was there something that you needed?"

Rinji sighed. "Are you trying to get rid of me? You don't seem very tired for someone who was about to go off to bed for the night. And you smell like perfume. Were you getting ready for a date?"

The Bending Branch

Taree sensed an unusual tension. Normally she and Rinji could sit and talk for hours. They also could sit, contently, in silence. But tonight he seemed edgy and restless. "A date?" she inquired, confused. "Oh, no, it's not perfume. It's bath beads." When Rinji didn't respond, she added, "I'm sorry I upset your parents. Your mom must think I'm useless."

"Why would you say that?" Rinji asked.

"I am useless when it comes to my family," Taree admitted.

Rinji grew irritated. "Don't judge my mom that way. She was just trying to make conversation. Your answers didn't really matter."

The Bending Branch

Taree sank even deeper into the love seat. "I didn't mean anything by it. It's just how it is. That's why I prefer to hang out with Matt's family."

"You still visit *his* family?" Rinji probed. "I thought you said he and you were just friends."

"I never really said that, but yes, we were just friends."

"You *were* deliberately ignoring me. How could you choose to put me through that? Do you know how many times I called?"

"I was *not* ignoring you. I fell asleep in the bath tub, okay? The visit today was overwhelming for me." She went on to explain. "I don't know what to do. My piano works beautifully, as it is, and it really only needs a tuning. Why should I risk restoring it? What it the restoration damages it?" Taree could no longer hold back the tears. "I have a German father who was rarely home and a mother who barely acknowledges my existence. I'm sorry I'm so flawed, okay? I did not choose my family. I can't change them. I am who I am."

Rinji was confused. Why was she behaving this way? He reached out to touch her hand, but she pulled it away and then moved off from the couch and went into the kitchen. "I think maybe you should go. I can't talk with you right now."

Rinji didn't want to leave. He'd never seen Taree so upset. What had he said that had set her off? What had his mom said? He started toward the kitchen.

The Bending Branch

"Please, Taree, I don't understand. What's wrong? How can I fix this?"

"Just go, okay. I'll be fine. I'm always fine. You can call me tomorrow. I promise I'll answer the phone. But, for tonight, please just go. I can't..."

Rinji did not turn to leave as Taree had expected. Instead, he wrapped his arms around her and dragged her into a hug. "I can't leave when you're this upset. We have to fix this."

Taree was at a loss for words. She stood, motionless, in the circle of his arms. She refused to talk for fear she would reveal too much.

Her plan was to begin building a wall—a wall that would eventually grow in thickness. By the time the wall was completed, he'd be far enough away that he'd never notice that she'd gone.

Yet here he stood, holding her tightly against his chest, refusing to allow her the room to build. Finally, she spoke: "Please let me go. Tonight I need my music."

Rinji drew her closer. Gently, he kissed her cheek. "Let me stay to listen and I'll agree to release you," he reasoned. "I won't let you shut me out. I want to share the friendship that you say you hold with your golden friend."

Taree pulled back but found she could not really move away. Her eyes met his. She could tell he was determined, possibly even angry. How could he not realize that he already knew that friendship? She pushed on him, trying to

The Bending Branch

gain some space. "I can't play for you," she insisted.

"It's your choice. If I leave now, I can't guarantee I'll be back. Play for me."

"Rinji, I . . ."

"No, Taree. Choose."

"I'm sorry, Rinji. I'm just not ready to share that kind of sorrow with you. It's an intimate part of me."

"I see," Rinji scoffed. "How presumptuous of me!"

She was suddenly standing alone and turned only in time to watch the door slam behind him. Sinking to her knees, she sobbed uncontrollably.

The Bending Branch

Chapter 14

The next morning, Taree made the most difficult decision of her life. First, she called her parents. She spoke briefly with her father who immediately agreed to help. He had wanted her to leave her present job for some time, but she had resisted because it gave her a feeling of independence. So, with the funds that she would need, she then wrote up her resignation and emailed it to her boss, giving the required, two-weeks' notice.

Next, she phoned her relatives in Germany. Her uncle had promised her a job at his factory if she ever needed one. She explained that she had completed her degree and that she wondered if he had something available in her field. She wanted to work for him throughout the summer in order to gain experience that would help her to get ahead in her career. Her uncle was thrilled to have her return to live with them, even for such a short time.

Next, she called her father's travel agent and arranged to buy the tickets. Her apartment lease had recently changed to month-to-month so she easily prepared a letter for that, as well. She would still need to rent a small storage unit, but that wouldn't be a problem at all.

Finally, she picked up the business card that Rinji's mom had left, and called his dad. When he did not answer, she left a brief, but irreversible message: "Hi,

The Bending Branch

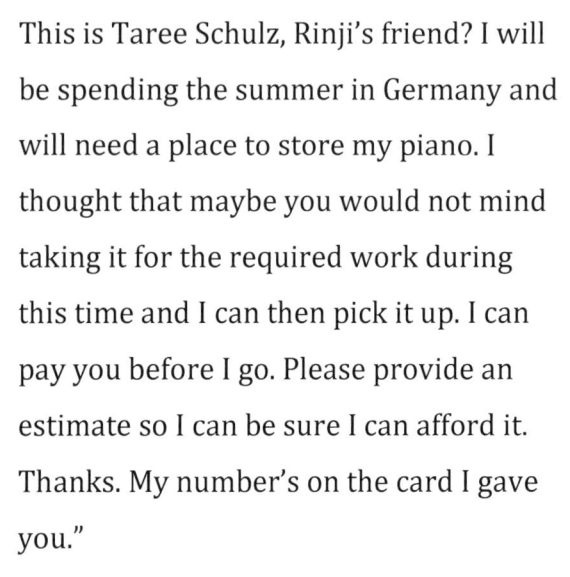

This is Taree Schulz, Rinji's friend? I will be spending the summer in Germany and will need a place to store my piano. I thought that maybe you would not mind taking it for the required work during this time and I can then pick it up. I can pay you before I go. Please provide an estimate so I can be sure I can afford it. Thanks. My number's on the card I gave you."

For some reason, Taree felt relieved. If all went as planned, she'd be on a plane in less than three weeks and using the degree that she had earned. She'd be gaining experience in her field and enjoying time with her relatives in Germany. She was glad that Rinji had stopped by the night before. She had needed a good kick in the pants.

The Bending Branch

Finally, she surfed the Internet and determined the best storage units to rent. She called the different options, made a decision, and then set up a unit in her name. She decided that she would begin to gather together boxes and tape, today. Then she could start to pack up whatever was not needed in order to continue to live.

The phone rang. "Hello?"

"Hi. My dad said that you called. He charges between three and five thousand dollars per refinished piano unless he requires parts for restoration. The tuning would be included. He thinks yours would cost in the three thousand range."

Rinji was all business. His voice was emotionless, as if he were speaking to a complete stranger. Although this stung,

The Bending Branch

Taree knew that she had made her decision. She responded, just as coolly: "Okay, thank you. Does that include pickup and delivery or do I need to arrange for that myself?"

"It's included but we need to set a date and time. You'll need to be there for paperwork and such."

"That's fine. He can pick it up as soon as he likes. It has to be soon, though. I leave for Germany in about three weeks."

Rinji paused. "I'll let him know," he stated. His voice was still flat.

"Thank you. Let me know when someone will be coming."

"Will do." Rinji hung up.

Taree wanted to call him back. She wanted to scream that he was supposed to realize that she had chosen him. Did he

The Bending Branch

not understand that she was placing her oldest and most trusted friend into his father's hands? Did he not see that she was finally stepping out from her secure, safe little world to at last risk all? How could he not understand this? Had she read between the lines and imagined words that were never there?

She phoned Matt's mom and was soon on her way to meet her at a coffee shop. Once there, they became immersed in conversation. An hour had passed when Taree's phone again rang. "Hello?"

"Can we talk?" It was Rinji.

"I'd like that," she admitted. "Um, I'm not home, though."

"When is a good time?"

"I'm at a coffee shop right now. Do you want to meet me here?"

The Bending Branch

"Talk at a coffee shop?"

"If you'd like. Or you decide where we should meet."

Rinji seemed to be growing impatient. "Come to my apartment when you can find the time and hopefully I'll be here." Then he hung up.

Taree ignored his outburst and spent a little longer with Matt's mom before they hugged and went their separate ways. Although she rarely went to Rinji's, she followed his instructions and headed out that way. She didn't like how his roommate flirted with her; it made her feel uncomfortable. But she left him a message on his phone and drove to his apartment anyway.

The Bending Branch

Chapter 15

"Rinji's not here. If you want, you can come in and wait."

Taree knew that this was not a good idea. Too often this roommate had left her feeling as if she were wearing nothing more than a thin layer of plastic wrap. She didn't feel safe. "No, that's okay. Please just tell him that I stopped by."

Could Rinji have done this deliberately? Had he planned for her to arrive when he wouldn't be there? Surely a friend would not behave this way. How had she managed to make such a mess of things?

The Bending Branch

She climbed back into her car, locking the doors straight away. Then she drove to a local hardware store, purchased boxes and other moving supplies, and returned home. She left all of the materials in the car and headed up the stairs to her apartment. When she arrived, Rinji was leaning against the hallway's wall. Had she misunderstood him? She was sure that she hadn't.

Ignoring him, she unlocked her apartment door and went in. He followed without an invitation.

Closing the door, he stood watching her. She continued to ignore him and put on a kettle of water to heat. Finally, she acknowledged his presence. "Will you be eating with me?"

The Bending Branch

Rinji remained where he was and did not speak. Why was he behaving this way?

Not knowing what else to do, Taree went to her piano, sat down, and began to play. She poured herself into the music, choosing a piece that she often played while drowning in tears. As she played, tears did begin to fill her eyes.

She played as if she were saying good-bye to him. When she finished, she dried her eyes with her sleeve and returned to the kitchen. Turning off the burner, she then moved to get a cup from the cupboard.

He finally spoke. "Why are you going to Germany?"

Taree remained calm. "I'm finally taking your advice. I'm moving forward in my life. I'm taking a risk. Besides, it's only three months."

"Taking a risk? Is someone waiting for you there?"

"You know there's not. Why are you so angry? I'm doing all you've challenged me to do."

"What does that mean?"

"You told me to choose."

"You're not making any sense."

Taree thought that she could say the same. Instead she asked, "Why did you send me to your apartment if you knew you were coming here?"

"I didn't know I was coming here. It's where I ended up when I couldn't stand waiting any longer."

"Now you're not making any sense."

The Bending Branch

Rinji crossed the room. Before she could even register how close they were, she found herself wrapped in a kiss. His lips were soft and firm at the same time. He was warm; his leather jacket was cold. She'd been caught off guard and was confused.

He searched her eyes and then tried again. This time she kissed him back. Her arms drew him closer, as if she couldn't bring him close enough. She clung to him. It seemed she sought to become a part of him. He deepened the kiss, not wanting to ever let go.

The cup fell off the counter and shattered. The couple was startled apart. A crimson blush rose to Taree's cheeks. She quickly turned, busying herself with the glass on the floor.

The Bending Branch

"Why are you running away from me?" he gently nudged.

"Your mom made it clear that you're off limits," Taree faltered. "I thought if I restored the piano, I might discover the identity of the smiling lady. If I can find my lost heritage, maybe your mom will change her mind."

"My parents do not choose my girl friends," Rinji bristled.

Taree ignored him. "I had a dream where she was humming to me—the song that I played for your parents. But I don't remember her. I don't know who she is. I want to know who I am—why I have a Japanese name. I've not really cared so much in the past... my ancestors do not make me who I am. But

The Bending Branch

it matters to your mom. She doesn't like me."

"She thought I gave you that song to play. She had the idea that I was trying to influence their response to you. She was angry that you played that song. She didn't like that you brought tears to my dad's eyes."

Taree finished cleaning up the glass and then took out a sweeper that uses disposable cleaning pads to ensure that there was not even a dusting left. She threw out the used cleaning pad, returned the sweeper to its corner and then washed her hands. "I'm sorry that I failed so miserably," she uttered. Rinji kissed her again.

Taree buried her face into his shoulder. "Please don't do that. You're going to make my stay in Germany insufferable. I have to do this. I have to conquer my fears."

Rinji smiled. "Insufferable, you say? Good. That is exactly how I already feel."

"Yeah, well, I didn't appreciate the visual undressing that I received from your roommate. I do hope that you didn't do that on purpose."

Rinji immediately showed concern. "He didn't touch you did he? I wasn't thinking that you'd go to my apartment. Why didn't you play for me last night? All of this could have been avoided."

"Hmm. If the kisses weren't part of last night's plans, then I think that I prefer how this played out today."

Rinji laughed. "You don't get another kiss until you've gone and come back then. I want you thinking of me every second of every day."

Taree smiled. "I know I will."

They had food delivered and ate together once more. When he left for home, Taree, for the first time, played the piano while filled with joy rather than sorrow.

Chapter 16

Taree sat at the airport, waiting for her plane. She had not seen or heard from Rinji since that night. But her piano was at his dad's shop, so at least she had that connection.

She was taking very little to Germany. She had a small carryon that also held her purse, and one, checked suitcase, mainly filled with clothes. She was looking forward to spending time with her second family and realized that she was thankful that they existed.

As she thought back to their first meeting, she recalled how different they were from her dad. She'd been integrated into the family and their chores, immediately. When she was gone at boarding school, they had visited her every weekend and had helped her with learning her German.

When school was out, they welcomed her back into their home with open arms. They believed that family was everything. All family members sat at dinner each night, not just on Fridays. And the atmosphere was one of true interest and genuine concern. It was all so different from the home that she had left behind.

Most baffling to her was her real parents' lack of communication. It was as if they had washed their hands of her and now merely had a monetary inconvenience. Yet she could never get any information about her parents. That

The Bending Branch

was one subject that her German relatives refused to discuss.

Boarding the plane, Taree could not help but feel disappointed. She had expected to at least find Rinji here, to see her off. But he never came. And now she was on the plane and about to disappear for the next three months.

Unconsciously, Taree touched her lips. Had she dreamed that Rinji had come that night? Had she imagined that he had kissed her? She knew he had, and it had all seemed so natural, but now she felt perplexed. As she stopped to think of him, she recognized that she could still conjure up the feel of his lips.

The flight was crowded. She was glad that she had an aisle seat. She remembered how embarrassed she had

The Bending Branch

been as a child. She had hated asking strangers to allow her out so that she could use the bathroom. She didn't really like to travel, especially alone.

She did enjoy visiting new places, however, and taking in the beauty of different cultures. She had learned to love Germany and had been saddened when she was told that she must return to a college in the States.

At the airport, she immediately recognized her uncle. This time he actually picked her up and swung her around. Her aunt had laughed. When Taree's feet were finally again on the floor, she was greeted by her, as well: "How's our little *Schwächling*? Do you still speak German?"

The Bending Branch

Taree was surprised at how quickly and smoothly her language switched over. She was speaking and understanding German almost immediately.

On the car ride home, she fell asleep. Her aunt woke her when they reached the house. "Who is Rinji, Love?" she asked.

Taree barely registered the question. "Oh, Rinji? How did you hear about him?" she finally managed.

"You said his name in your sleep. How is Matthew? Does he still write you?"

"I'm sorry, *Tante (ton-tuh)*. I thought I told you. Matt died during my freshman year at college."

The Bending Branch

"Oh, that is too bad. Well, these things happen, don't they? He seemed like such a nice boy."

Taree was relieved that she didn't have to explain who Rinji was. Her aunt seemed to have forgotten that she'd asked.

The rest of the day was a blur of cousins, food preparation and chores. To Taree, it felt as if she had never left. There were fewer children at home, but the routines and the schedules all appeared to have remained the same. She was surprised that she found it so comforting.

Finally, when it was almost time for bed, she was called into the den to speak with her father. He had mainly wanted to be sure that the trip had gone well and

The Bending Branch

that she had made it there safely and without incident. Yet only one statement stuck in her mind: "Don't humiliate me, Taree," he had said, "they're the only family I've got."

The Bending Branch

Chapter 17

As the summer came to a close, Taree's uncle joked about keeping her there and refusing to allow her to go home. She thought about Rinji and how he had not contacted her the entire time she was gone. She had broken down and called him only once, but he hadn't been home. She had hung up without having left a message. His roommate had not recognized her voice and had immediately stated that Rinji was out with Heather. She had tried not to think of it and did her best to give him the benefit of the doubt. She could no longer imagine the feel of his lips.

The Bending Branch

Now it was time to go home. She had a fabulous, six-figure job waiting for her. Her uncle had sent resumes to all of his American connections and colleagues. She had even managed to stay near to her old town.

She hugged her cousins, aunt, and uncle good-bye and then boarded the plane. She hadn't called anyone to get her. She had decided to take a shuttle to a hotel, spend the night, and then just lease a car so she could drive herself home.

The entire first half of the trip was spent listening to a grade-school girl who wanted to share her summer project. Taree did her best to feign interest and to smile whenever she thought it to be appropriate. Finally, she was able to break free and change seats when the

The Bending Branch

girl's mom insisted that her daughter take a bathroom break.

Taree moved to the back of the plane, freshened up in the bathroom, and then sat down in an empty row of seats. She hadn't noticed the man who was sitting across the aisle. He was probably about ten years her senior. Taree hoped that he would show no interest in conversation.

"Aren't you Taree Schulz?" he asked.

Taree turned to look at him. "Yes, but . . ."

"You'd know me as Mr. Healy," he provided.

Taree couldn't believe it. "Mr. Healy? From the fifth grade? How'd you recognize me?"

"I still have all of my fifth grade, class photos," he explained.

The Bending Branch

"I see," voiced Taree. She was immediately annoyed with herself for sounding like Rinji.

"So where has your life taken you?" he continued. "Besides Germany, that is," he added.

"Um, not far at all, really. I'm on my way back to my fifth grade's quaint little town."

"Well, it was nice to see you again. I've got to get back to grading these papers. Kids today don't have the talent that I sensed in you. Anyway, I wish you the very best."

"Thank you, Mr. Healy. You, too."

Taree asked the flight attendant for a pillow and then closed her eyes for the remainder of the trip. She wondered if her teacher had confused her with someone else. Talented? She'd never received above a B+.

Seeing Mr. Healy had brought back memories of Matt. He seemed so distant now. She was even having difficulty remembering his face. A tear formed in the corner of her eye, so she callously brushed it away.

Once at the airport, Taree wasted no time in picking up her luggage. She had returned with an extra bag. As she rolled her luggage in front of her, her carryon and purse bounced against her sides. When she arrived at the information booth, she asked the attendant about the shuttle. It had never occurred to her that the shuttle would not be available. She was told that the rental station might still

The Bending Branch

be open and that if she hurried she might be able to lease a car, instead.

Taree made it to the rental station just in time to watch as the employee locked it up for the night. With a deep sigh, she sat down on a nearby bench and pulled out her cell phone. Someone sat down on the other end of the bench just as the phone began to ring. The bench swerved loose, causing Taree to drop the phone and to lose her balance. She went sprawling onto the ceramic floor. The woman on the other end of the bench quickly stood up and left.

A janitor came running to her assistance. He picked up her now-broken phone and helped her to rise, carefully, to her feet. Then he walked with her to the claims department so she could report

The Bending Branch

the accident and any losses. Taree thanked him and he left.

The claims person had her fill out a packet of forms and provided her with copies. Then she allowed her to use the phone. Taree had no choice but to call her parents. It was now late into the night and the town was a good three hours away. "Dad," Taree managed, "I'm at the airport. A bench broke and I had a bit of a fall. Do you think that you and mom could come get me? They want me to visit the hospital, as well."

"Your mom and I have separated and I really can't get away at the moment. Could you maybe call her instead? She has a new number, though. Do you have it?" Taree could hear a young woman giggling in the background.

The Bending Branch

"Never mind, Dad. I'll call one of my friends," Taree responded. She hung up the phone. "I'll need to call someone else," she informed the airport employee.

"Sure, Hon," the lady said, dismissively.

After two more calls, Taree had no one left to try except Rinji. She really didn't want to call him but felt she had no choice. He answered on the first ring.

"Hello?"

"Hi Rinji, it's Taree," she began. "I'm kind of stuck at the airport and wondered if maybe you might be able to get me?"

"You're at the airport? Why didn't you tell me you were coming home today! Of course I'll come get you. Which airport and where?"

The Bending Branch

Taree provided all of the details, telling him where to meet her and that her cell phone was broken; she then hung up the phone. He had sounded so happy to hear from her. Had she misjudged him? She was in too much pain to care. She thanked the lady, took the additional forms that the hospital would need, and headed for the designated restaurant.

Three hours later, Rinji arrived. He was about to hug her when she quickly told him not to, and why. He scanned her for bruises and saw that both of her arms were scraped up. He couldn't tell what her legs looked like because they were encased in jeans. "Are you okay?" he queried.

The Bending Branch

"I think so," she answered. "Not the best welcome to America, though."

"Why didn't you tell me you were coming home today? I could have been here waiting for you. All of this could have been avoided."

His last sentence brought her back to a different time. Without thinking, she relayed this memory in her response: "Well, this time, I think that avoidance would have been a good thing. I don't like how this played out."

Rinji smiled. Gently, he leaned down and planted a kiss on her forehead. "Neither do I. It left you way too fragile," he teased.

Although she didn't want to change his playful mood, she had to ask. "Who's Heather?"

The Bending Branch

Rinji scowled. "How'd you hear about Heather?" he wondered.

"Your roommate told me you were out with her the one time I called."

"You called? Hmm, I see," Rinji seemed a bit annoyed.

"Never mind, you don't have to tell me. I just need to get . . ." Taree suddenly realized that she had nowhere to go.

"Taree? What's wrong? Do you hurt?"

"Yes, but it's not that. I just realized that I don't have a home; I have nowhere to go."

"Then come with me. You can meet Heather. She's the roommate's newest acquisition. She follows me everywhere I go, at his request. It's extremely irritating. I'm in the process of buying

The Bending Branch

myself a house so I can finally escape. But it's all still in progress."

Taree tried to hide how happy she was to find out that Heather was not only his roommate's interest, but that she also aggravated him. She didn't want to sound too indifferent. "Go with *you*?" she asked. "I'm not sure that's a good idea."

"I thought you trusted me."

"I do trust you."

"Then come with me. Did you say that we need to stop off at the hospital first? There's one on our route."

"The airport wants me to, but I'm so tired."

"But that could be a symptom. Come on; we'll go together." And with that, Rinji took Taree's bags and they both headed to his car.

The Bending Branch

Chapter 18

About an hour later, Rinji parked at the hospital. Although he tried not to make it obvious, he had been attempting to keep the conversation going so that Taree would not fall asleep. He was worried that she might have a concussion even though her pupils appeared to be okay.

As they walked into the hospital, Taree dug into her handbag so she'd have the airport papers to present. She was thankful that the janitor had seen what had happened since it seemed rather an incredulous story.

Rinji stayed with her as much as possible. When the nurses were going to

The Bending Branch

send him away, Taree begged that they allow him to stay. When they said only family could be present, Rinji asked if a fiancé counted as family. When the nurses allowed him to remain, Taree thanked him for his thoughtfulness. She did not want to be alone.

Rinji insisted that he, also, did not want to leave her alone. He was glad that she approved. It soon became clear why they were trying to separate them, however. It was as if no one had read the report or seen the forms that she had submitted. They thought she was a battered woman!

Finally, she was able to get someone to listen. This person called the airport and spoke to the janitor who saw the whole thing. The janitor took pictures of

The Bending Branch

the bench and sent them to the hospital, along with a statement.

Taree felt terrible that they thought Rinji would ever harm her. She moved closer to him and snuggled herself against his arm. He looked down, reassuring her with a smile. The nurses who saw this tender scene no longer had the nagging doubts of abuse.

After many x-rays, and even more doctors, she was released. Her wounds were superficial and looked a lot worse than they actually were. As they left the hospital, Taree suddenly stopped. Rinji halted beside her, confused. "I almost ran into you. What's wrong?"

She turned to face him. "My wounds are only on the surface and I'm loaded with pain medicine. I've decided that I

The Bending Branch

want a proper greeting, Akiyama Rinji." Her eyes sparkled with challenge.

Rinji slid his arms around her waist and drew her close to himself. "Just how proper are we talking?" he chuckled. "*British* proper? Or do you mean?" he didn't get to finish his sentence. Taree had stopped his words with a playful kiss.

The mischievous had soon bloomed into intense passion. When Rinji finally lifted his head, they both were out of breath. As their eyes locked, Taree refused to allow hers to waver. She wanted this man and she was not going to leave room for him to have any doubts about how she felt.

Rinji was the one to break the spell. "We should go," he suggested. He moved

The Bending Branch

away and offered her his hand, which she promptly took.

Once in the car again, Taree fell silent. For some reason, she still had a nagging feeling that she had imposed herself on him. She began to stare out the window.

Rinji broke the stillness. "Do your parents know that you're back?"

Taree didn't know how to answer. At last she said, "I called my dad before I called you. He informed me that he and mom are separated and that I should call her, instead. He offered to give me her number, but she's always been the more indifferent of the two so I told him to forget about it and hung up. I guess his date was of higher concern."

"He was on a date? And he put her before you?"

The Bending Branch

"Well, I'd rather think it was a date than consider the other possibilities. A rather young woman was giggling in the background."

"Did he know you were hurt?"

"That's the second thing I told him. I said I was at the airport and that I had fallen. He didn't seem too concerned."

"I'm sorry. You had no idea they were having problems?"

"They've always had problems. I guess I just never considered that they'd stop dealing with them. It's fine, though. I have my family in Germany. I have Matt's family here. And I have good friends like you."

"Friend, you say? Did we not decide I was more than that? I thought we agreed

The Bending Branch

I was your fiancé." Rinji's eyes were dancing. "Well?"

"That was for the nurses' benefit," Taree countered, also in an impish voice. "I know that you can't possibly want to really be seen as part of my family."

Rinji pulled into the next rest area and came to a stop. "Who says I have to be part of *your* family?" he teased. "You're the one who would be changing her last name." He got out from the car and headed into the building. Taree followed.

When they returned to the car, Rinji became serious. "Did you miss me, Taree? I didn't get any letters."

"Well, neither did I."

"True. I didn't know what to write."

The Bending Branch

"Me neither. But I thought about you every second of every day. I sometimes ached for you."

Rinji reached over and gently stroked her cheek. "I wanted you to ache for me," he admitted.

"I know you did. And I do."

Rinji breathed in a deep breath of satisfaction. "Good," was all he said.

The Bending Branch

Chapter 19

The next morning, Taree walked out from Rinji's room, wearing his sweatshirt and pants. Rinji followed directly behind, his hand in hers, as if being led. The look on his roommate's face was well worth the deception. After the roommate had left for the day, Taree and Rinji broke out in festive, triumphant laughter.

Although Taree had accepted Rinji's offer for a place to stay the night, she knew that Rinji did not believe in going all the way before marriage. He knew that neither did she. They had talked numerous times about being responsible and valuing relationships. He also had a very comfortable couch in his room,

The Bending Branch

along with a bed. Besides, it was worth it if it got rid of the unwanted advances of his roommate.

They spent the day looking at apartments. Taree had planned to do this alone, but Rinji insisted that he wanted to spend time with her. She was amazed that she found an apartment that she liked in just one day. She would even be able to move in as early as Monday.

Rinji worried it would be too expensive. She had not yet told him of her new job. Her new employers had even written in a two-week adjustment period for her to get resettled. She suddenly realized that she was afraid he'd pull away. What if she earned more than he did? She knew it shouldn't matter, but she also knew that, for some men, regardless of how hard they tried to behave as if it didn't, it did.

She forced herself to face this fear straight on. After all, he was buying a house, right? "I know it seems expensive, but I'm presently single, the place is energy efficient, and I have an actual job in my field—an actual job, Rinji. Aren't you proud of me? No more scraping together bottles or cans for change."

Rinji smiled. "I am proud of you. But I always have been, haven't I? Even when you were supposed to get a salary but instead became more of a volunteer than an employee."

"Yes, but it bothered you that I allowed them to take advantage of me. Should I keep looking, then? You are usually right about these things."

The Bending Branch

"I think you can get the same thing for less, yes. But you're the one who has to live with whatever you choose. A townhome is for rent about two blocks from the house I am buying, though. Would you like to try there, first?"

"Are you sure you want me to live that close?"

"What do you think?" He lightheartedly gave her the once-over while grinning sheepishly.

Taree blushed. "I'm sorry I asked," she laughed.

"But you're not. Not really." Rinji kissed her, shamelessly.

And Taree had to admit, he was right. She was not sorry that she had asked. She liked the way that he looked at her, talked to her, smiled at her, and appreciated her. But most of all, she savored his kisses. "I think I'll like any place that could put me closer to you," she reasoned. So they decided to check it out after they stopped and had lunch.

The townhome had two levels. Upstairs was a master bedroom with a master bath and walk-in closet. The downstairs had a living room, kitchen, den, full bath, dining room, and second bedroom. It would probably cost more to heat and cool, but it was also two hundred dollars less per month.

Furthermore, it required only a six-month lease at the same rate as a one-year lease and then would automatically stay the same price from month-to-month unless the landlord gave sixty-days notice of the increase. She also

The Bending Branch

would have the option to sign for another six months to a year if she preferred, and she only needed to give thirty-days notice if she decided she wanted to move once the lease had completed. It almost seemed too good to be true. It was definitely larger than the earlier apartment, but it was also older and not energy efficient.

Yet it did come with a walk-in garage. The apartment only offered an open lot to park in.

"Rinji, what do you think?" she asked.

"If it were me, I'd take it," he admitted. "The other apartment had a small leak that would need to be repaired but it appears that this owner takes good care of his property."

The Bending Branch

Taree turned to the real estate agent. "Can I get all the details in writing and call you?" she asked.

The real estate agent obliged and Rinji and Taree were soon headed back out to his car. "By the way, where's your car?" Rinji wondered.

"It's at my dad's house. I'm supposed to pick it up tomorrow. I kind of hope he's gone when I get there, though. I don't really want to meet anyone he might be dating."

"Yeah, I can understand that. Do you have a ride to get there? I'd love to help, but tomorrow I have to work."

"My mom's going to take me because she also has a key. I've not seen her since I've been back. Dad had told me to ask her since she's been complaining about

The Bending Branch

needing something she left behind. She agreed, anyway. The day should be interesting, to say the least."

"Yeah. Well, good luck with that. So, where to? Are you staying again with me?"

"Um . . . not if you don't want me to. I mean, you have to work tomorrow. I could call my mom to see if I can stay there."

"Are you okay with that?"

"Yeah, so long as she is. Oh, can I use your phone? I forgot that mine's still broken."

"Let's go to my place to eat and you can call her from there. My phone's in my pocket and it's probably not a good idea for you to fish for it while I'm driving."

Taree blushed again. "Okay. Sounds good."

The Bending Branch

Chapter 20

Once it was settled, Rinji drove Taree out to her mom's place and dropped her off. As he helped her to carry in her cases, her mom basically stayed out of the way. There were no questions, no interferences, nor any other interruptions.

When it came time for Rinji to leave, Taree walked him out to the car. She hugged him good night and turned to go back up to her mom's. He immediately sensed that she was avoiding a kiss. Before she could leave, he asked her a question. "Is your mom always this noninvasive, or is this her way of making me feel unwelcome?"

The Bending Branch

"She rarely involves herself in my life. She neither likes, nor dislikes you." Taree changed the subject. "Do *you* think she looks Japanese?"

"No. Not really. But neither does your dad."

Taree seemed pensive. "I know, right? So why do I have a Japanese name? It's unlikely that it's due to any heritage, right?"

"Does it matter?"

"Doesn't it? Your mom already dislikes me."

"So?"

"She obviously disapproves. Don't pretend it doesn't bother you. You are so close to your parents, your family. You'd never want to hurt any of them, least of all, your mom."

"So what are you saying, exactly?"

"Nothing: I'm not saying anything."

The Bending Branch

"I think you are."

"Maybe I am. I love you, Rinji. I don't want to be the reason that you feel anguish or pain. Maybe I should have stayed away."

"Maybe you should have. It's obvious that you neither trust, nor believe in me. You shouldn't make assumptions based on the little you've observed."

"I'm sorry. I didn't mean to . . ."

"I've got to go."

"Are you angry? Please don't be angry."

"I'm not. I just need to go. I have a long day tomorrow. I've got to get up at four."

"Okay, then," Taree returned, unconvinced. "Thanks for everything. I'll see you tomorrow."

Rinji did not reply; he hopped into his car and left. And Taree could not help but notice—she'd told Rinji that she loved him.

The Bending Branch

He did not say it back. She knew why, too . . . he wouldn't say it; not unless he knew it to be true.

The Bending Branch

Chapter 21

After crying herself to sleep, with her face muffled next to her pillow, Taree awoke with a feeling of emptiness. She should have known it was too early to mention his mom's rejection and she should never have confessed her love for him. How was it that her mother could evoke such a sense of insecurity in her that it would cause her to sabotage such a promising relationship?

Taree treated her eyes, to hide the puffiness, and then took a shower. Once dressed, she applied a second treatment, added her makeup, and then headed downstairs. She found her mom to be as unreliable as always. There was a note on the table: *Sorry, Taree. Forgot I had a commitment this morning. I should be back by one but feel free to go to your dad's without me. I found what I thought I had left behind. Here's the key. Mom.*

Taree remembered that Matt's younger sister would have the day off, so decided to call her. Narissa made it clear that she would only be able to help with the car as she had already planned a day with her boy friend. Taree thanked her and told her that so long as she had her car, then all would be well. Narissa had laughed and said that she completely understood. Taree told her to meet her at the bakery that was at the corner of the street.

Getting into the car, Taree remembered how much Narissa resembled Matt. They had often pretended to be twins when he was alive. She was as feminine as Matt was masculine, yet their eyes held a visible joy for life. They hugged and then Narissa inquired, "Which way, Sis?"

The warmth that Narissa showed began to disperse the emptiness that had crept into Taree's heart. She gave Narissa the address for the GPS and they were soon off to get her car. After making sure that Taree was able to start the car, that it had enough gas, that the registration, inspection, and insurance were all up to date, and that it started, Narissa hugged her good-bye and took off to meet her boy friend. Taree had not been surprised to find that her car had been cared for so completely, for that was the personality of her dad. She waved as Narissa sped off.

She then shut off the engine, locked the doors, and went into the garage to be sure she had everything. A spare tire leaned

The Bending Branch

against the wall. It had a piece of paper attached: *Put this in your trunk, Taree. Leave the donut here. I told you to never settle for a donut.*

Taree went out to her car, unlocked the trunk, removed the limited-use, spare tire, and then carried it into the garage. She set it next to the normal-size tire and then picked up this tire to take it back out to her trunk. She then strapped this tire in, as her father had taught her, since it would not fit where the smaller spare had been. Next, she closed her trunk and went back to lock up the garage.

Now she was on her way to return her mother's key. It was a little after one.

When she arrived, she could tell her mother was not yet home. She also realized that she did not have a key for her mother's

The Bending Branch

place. She scribbled a note on a sticky pad and then stuck it to her mother's door, just under the door knob. Here, she had learned, the note was blocked by the screen door and could not be seen from the road. She'd just have to keep the key for now.

Taree returned to her car, locked the doors, and sat quietly in the driver's seat. She closed her eyes. Matt's face immediately took shape. He had been so supportive. His smile had always been infectious. She decided she would take the townhome. She needed a place for her things.

She drove out to her storage unit and went inside. Here she took down a banker's box, sat on one of the chairs, opened the box, and took out a folder. She lifted out the picture that Matt had drawn of the mysterious woman and hugged it to her chest. Then she

The Bending Branch

returned it to the box and pulled out a stack of letters; they were held together by a rubber band. One by one, she began to read.

By the time she had finished, tears were slowly sliding down her cheeks. She had not realized it at the time, but Matt loved her. She had not been able to share those feelings. She had been a shell at the time. Yet he still remained her friend and had been patiently waiting.

Taree carefully stacked them back into a pile and replaced the rubber band. She returned them to the box. Standing to her feet, she returned the box to its place in the storage unit.

As she locked the unit back up, she had a renewed hope. She climbed back into her car and drove to her carrier's closet cell phone shop. Here she renewed her contract for

The Bending Branch

another two years and bought the phone at the top of the line. Now people could call her again. She checked her messages, relieved that her new employer had not tried to contact her, and then she went back out and drove away.

At the nearby mall, she ate a small lunch and left a message for the real estate lady. Then she went into her favorite salon and asked if they had time to do a makeover. Her stylist was thrilled to finally be given this chance; she'd been telling Taree that her look was outdated for ages!

A refined, elegant Taree left the salon. She had a new way to apply her makeup, new colors that brought out her features, and a trendy haircut that made her appear confident. She now carried a sexy vibe, of which, she was totally unaware. Adding this

The Bending Branch

to her already fashionable wardrobe, Taree was now the picture of success.

Returning to her car, she decided to try her mom again. She locked her doors and then phoned her mother. They agreed to meet at the house in an hour for dinner and to make plans from there.

Taree was surprised when she got a return call from the realtor. She'd never had a realtor call her on a Sunday. She answered her phone. "Hello?"

"Miss Schulz? Would you be able to meet me now? Tomorrow starts the first of the month and the owner prefers the rent to be due on this day. Would you mind?"

Taree told her that it was a perfect time to meet and then drove out to the realtor's office. With the unused portion of money that her dad had provided for Germany, she wrote

The Bending Branch

the necessary checks and then signed all of the papers. Once she received the copies, along with the keys, she thanked the lady and then drove to the nearest department store. Here she bought an air mattress and then, realizing the time, she drove on over to her mother's.

The Bending Branch

Chapter 22

Unpredictably, Taree's mother said nothing about her daughter's new look. This caused Taree to forget she'd done anything out of the ordinary. And for the first time, they actually had a good visit. Her mother even told her to keep her father's key.

When it was time to leave, Taree loaded her luggage into her car and then waved good-bye to her mother. She then drove to her new residence and parked in the walk-in garage. Locking the garage door, she then went in through the adjoining door and into her townhome's kitchen.

Here she moved on upstairs and set up the air mattress. As she allowed it to blow itself up, she returned to her car for the luggage.

The Bending Branch

Finally, she shut down the pump only to realize she'd forgotten to ask her mother if she could borrow some bedding.

It was too late at night to return to the store. Besides, that bedding would need washing for her to use it. She'd always had sensitive skin and knew that the chemicals would leave her sleepless. She called her mom, but there was no answer.

Next, she called her dad. He had just arrived home and said he would be glad to loan her the sheets and blankets that she needed. So, she unlocked her garage door, climbed back into her car, used the remote to open the door, pulled out, and then remotely shut the door once more. She was glad to note that the remote had a scrambler so that the signal could not be easily copied.

The Bending Branch

Once at her dad's, she went up to the door and rang the bell. He immediately commented on her new look: "Now that's the look of professionalism, Taree. It's about time you became serious. I'm thankful you've chosen to uphold my brother's reputation." Then he reverted to his cool self and bid her a good night.

Taree thanked him, took the bedding, and headed back out to the car. It was close to midnight when she again arrived home. She parked the car in the garage, shut the door with the remote, and then went inside.

As she prepared the airbed, her phone rang. It was Rinji. "I thought you said I'd see you yesterday," he stated.

Taree looked down at her watch. "I'm sorry. The day was kind of busy."

The Bending Branch

"And the night, too?" he continued. His voice was cold. She wondered why he had bothered to call.

"I was with my mom," she answered.

"All day *and* night?" he interrogated.

"No, I guess not. But in the morning, *yes*, and again at night. I'm sorry I didn't think to call."

"No you're not. You wanted *me* to call *you*, so you waited."

Taree was saddened that he thought she was that petty. She didn't really know how to answer him. "I've had a very long day, Rinji. It was less stressful than I expected, but it was long, none-the-less. I am sorry I didn't call you. It really was not intentional as you seem to think."

The Bending Branch

Rinji blew out air. "Well, no matter. My dad wants you to know that your piano is finished."

Taree was glad that she had paid Rinji's dad before she left. She had drained her savings, but she had paid him $3500.00 before she had gone to Germany. He had said that it was more than he was expecting but she had insisted. "Oh. Tell him I will call him tomorrow and let him know where it can be delivered."

"No. He wants to see you at his shop. He says you paid him too much and he also has something important to show you on the piano, itself." Rinji perceived a deliberate attempt to not tell him where she was, but he decided to ignore it: he was not going to play this game. But her next flow of words crushed both of his theories.

The Bending Branch

"I almost forgot," she shared. "Thank you for telling me about the townhome. I signed the lease and am staying here tonight, or rather this morning," she giggled. "So far I've only got an airbed—oh, and my luggage—but I'm hoping to move the rest of my stuff in before the end of the week. I appreciate the help you gave in making my decision."

So she hadn't purposely ignored him? She wasn't playing games? Rinji was puzzled. "You're welcome," he said, his voice noticeably softening.

"Oh, I got a makeover, too, and the strangest thing happened . . . my mom didn't say anything while my dad actually liked it. I hope you'll like it," she added, shyly.

Rinji was sorry now that he'd waited to hear from her and hadn't called her sooner. He sensed that she and he had taken a few

The Bending Branch

steps backwards because of his obstinacy. He should have believed in her; he should not have grouped her with petty girls and women from his past. "How could I not?" he assured her. "You like it, right? That's what's important."

Taree smiled. "Yes, I think I do," she decided. "My dad's right. I now have the look of success."

Rinji wanted to go see her. At the same time, though, he had to work in less than four hours. "Well, I need to get some sleep if I'm going to rise for work at four," he reasoned.

"Yes, I'd say that's a good idea," Taree agreed. "Good night, Rinji," she breathed.

"Good night, Taree. Sleep well." He hung up before she could answer.

The Bending Branch

Chapter 23

The next day, Taree rose early; she wanted to call Rinji to see if she could go eat with him before he headed off to work. She called his phone.

"Hello? Taree?"

"Hi Rinji," she answered. "I thought maybe you wouldn't mind some company for breakfast?"

"Really? But it's not even four."

"I know, but I didn't get to see you yesterday and I just wanted to be sure that everything's okay."

"I'll stop over on my way to work, then," he insisted. "I don't really have good breakfast options here today."

The Bending Branch

Taree felt mildly rejected, but she tried not to reveal this in her voice. "Okay. I'll see you then." She hung up. She expected he wouldn't stop over for at least half an hour since she'd awakened him, so she actually jumped when the door bell rang in just under ten minutes.

She went to the door, peered out the peephole, and then let him in. Before she could say anything, he drew her into his arms and gave her an extremely gentle kiss. She quickly responded but then tenderly pulled away.

Rinji appeared to have showered and then come directly over to see her. This made her feel badly; she had tried not to convey her disappointment. She hadn't wanted to manipulate him. She was about to apologize when he kissed her again.

The Bending Branch

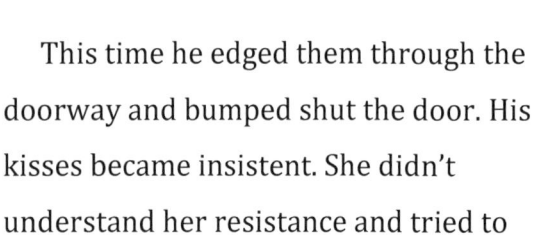

This time he edged them through the doorway and bumped shut the door. His kisses became insistent. She didn't understand her resistance and tried to concentrate on the sensation of his lips and the smell of his skin. He stepped back. "Why are you fighting me, Taree? Isn't this what you wanted?"

Taree was baffled. "I . . . I . . . I don't know."

Rinji, she could tell, was frustrated. His next words only solidified this observation: "Stop sending me mixed signals: one minute you want to be friends; the next minute you're kissing me as if we're already lovers; then you kiss me, shyly, as if I'm nothing more than a schoolgirl crush; and finally, you push me away again."

"You're right." Taree agreed. "I'm being totally unfair. I think, for now, you should forget about me. I'm obviously a mess at the moment and you deserve better than that. I guess I'll call you when I sort things out and hope that you've not moved on and are no longer interested."

Rinji opened his mouth to interrupt, but Taree rushed onward, "I'm sorry I've hurt you. I value you and your friendship more than anything. So, while I'm thinking clearly, please just go."

Rinji refused. Instead, he dialed his phone. "Hi, this is Rinji. Yeah, I'm not coming in to work today. Definitely, not a problem, I should be back tomorrow. Thanks." Then he turned to Taree. "You and I are going to talk."

Taree moved to the stairs and sat down. She was angry with herself and annoyed with Rinji. Tears began to slide down her face. "I'm sorry," she managed.

The Bending Branch

"Come," he insisted. He raised her to her feet and moved them up the stairs. "I think we could both use some sleep before we work this out."

Taree surrendered and followed him up the stairs. He sat on the edge of her airbed and pulled her down next to him. Then he quietly explained that he would stay with her, holding her in his arms as she slept. He moved them onto the bed and she immediately snuggled against him, burying her face into his neck. She repeated, "I'm sorry."

He kissed her forehead. "Don't be. Just sleep, okay?"

The Bending Branch

Chapter 24

Taree awoke in Rinji's arms and remembered what an embarrassment she had been. She tried to move out from the circle of his arms without disturbing him, but he immediately drew her closer once more. "Please don't go," he said.

She looked over at him and was suddenly overwhelmed by her feelings. She now understood why she had behaved the way she did.

She had finally been freed from Matt's memory and had recognized that she no longer had a path to follow. The path had merged with the garden. She had panicked because her love for Rinji had integrated itself with her life. She couldn't imagine her

The Bending Branch

life without him. She loved Rinji more than she loved life. She again tried to move away.

"Taree, please stay."

She forced herself to meet his eyes. "For how long, Rinji?" she asked, pointedly.

"For always," he breathed.

She couldn't resist him any longer. She did not want to live without him and refused to let her fear try to protect her from possible future pain . . . she had to risk that they would really be forever. She turned toward him and pressed her lips against his. "I love you," she whispered.

"I know," he answered. "And I love you." He then accepted her kiss with a response that only encouraged her to kiss him more.

After some time had passed, Taree again apologized. Then she went on to explain her earlier trepidation. "Rinji, I want to explain."

The Bending Branch

"There's no need, Taree. We were both tired. It's . . . "

"There is a need, though. I need you to know this so that you will always fight your way back to me. Like you did today."

"Okay. If it's that important, then I'll listen."

"Thank you. I appreciate that." She stopped to hug him. When she received back his assuring squeeze, she began. "Over the years I've developed the ability to shut myself down whenever I feel emotionally out of control, or threatened. Once I realized that this could get in the way of my happiness, I began to struggle to overcome this ability. The first hurdle was when I accepted help from Matt in the fifth grade. I had to admit that my capacity for anything creative or imaginative had been severely diminished

The Bending Branch

and trust Matt to help me find what little of it remained. It was one of the scariest, yet one of the most rewarding, things I have ever done. As Matt and I became friends, I learned to prevail over this automatic shutdown for the majority of things in my life."

Taree looked over at Rinji to be sure he was listening. "Go on," he encouraged.

"Well, on the night that I told you that I love you, and you became so incredibly unresponsive, I hadn't meant to share this with you. I guess it was fresh in my mind because it's a totally new awareness for me; I'd only just recognized that I loved you on the day that your parents came to look at my piano. I realized that love had grown up around me as if a garden surrounding life's path. It was nothing like the falling that fairy tales had prepared me for. I realized that you had replaced my golden piano and when I felt threatened—that your mother was not even trying to like me—I panicked. Fear began to insist on protecting me."

She paused, catching her breath. Her eyes quickly scanned Rinji to be sure that her mentioning his mother had not caused him to stop listening. Assured that he hadn't, she continued. "This morning, when you surprised me by coming straight over after I had called, it threw me off balance. My walls immediately rose; this ability to shut myself down took over. My body froze while my mind battled for control. I didn't understand this protective response at the time, but now I do. Rinji, I no longer have a path that travels through this garden; the path has merged with the garden and I cannot imagine a life without you."

The Bending Branch

At first, Rinji was speechless. He just pulled Taree closer, reassuring her. Slowly, he spoke, "Taree, I never had a path through the garden; the path and garden merged on the day we met. You have always intrigued me; I loved you the moment we became friends." He kissed her.

Taree smiled. "Don't ever let me push you away or shut you out."

"That's why I'm here today," Rinji reminded her, and he kissed her again. "Okay, it's time to head out. My dad insisted that he wanted to see you, today. He wouldn't tell me anything but he seemed excited about your refinished piano."

"Rinji, I'm a bit nervous about that."

"But you'll have me with you," he reasoned.

"Always, right?"

The Bending Branch

"Right."

"Then let's go."

The Bending Branch

Chapter 25

Rinji's dad was waiting for them when they arrived. "Hello, Mr. Akiyama," Taree greeted.

Mr. Akiyama gave her a warm smile. "Hello, Miss Schulz," he answered. "I have something beautiful to show you!"

"Yes, Rinji told me so. What did you find on my piano that is so beautiful, Sir?"

"Come, Taree. Let me show you."

Taree and Rinji followed his dad into the next room. The piano gleamed in beautiful cherry. It was magnificent! Taree was amazed. "Mr. Akiyama, it's glorious!" she exclaimed.

The Bending Branch

Rinji's dad shone with pride. "And that's not the entire story, Miss Schulz. Open the lid."

Taree moved over to the piano and opened the lid. The face of the mysterious lady looked back at her. Next to the face was an inscription in Japanese. "It's the woman from my dreams," Taree gasped. "Does it say who she is?"

Rinji's dad came closer. It says, "To my beautiful granddaughter, Taree. I send my piano in my place. Live well in America. Remember that I love you, Kazue (*kah-zoo-EH*)."

Taree had to sit down. "So she *was* my grandmother. But why would my parents hide this from me?"

Mr. Akiyama frowned. "I know it is difficult, child, but try not to judge them too

The Bending Branch

harshly. There might be a reason that is unknown. There is a Japanese proverb: 'Everyone makes mistakes. That's why there is an eraser on every pencil.'"

"Thank you, Sir," Taree acknowledged. "Maybe they gave me the piano for this reason. The gold paint really did not do it justice, did it? You've worked a true miracle. I wonder, though, if my grandmother was Japanese, why is her piano a Steinway & Sons? Do I owe you any money, Sir?"

"No, Miss. You paid me $250.00 too much."

"How can that be?"

"The paint, once I tested it, proved to not be so much a problem. It seemed as if someone had always planned for it to come off."

"I see. Well, when can I have it delivered?"

The Bending Branch

"Now, if you like. Rinji can go with you and the men."

"Thank you, Sir. I appreciate all you've done."

"You are welcome, Taree. I'll get the men."

With his dad out of the room, Rinji gently rubbed Taree's shoulder. She smiled up at him and then he went to help his father. His mother came into the room.

"Hello, Miss Schulz," she acknowledged. "Will it be okay if I come with you to your home? I still will need to tune your piano."

"I would be honored if you have the time. Thank you."

"Are you okay, Miss Schulz?"

"Yes, Ma'am. And my piano is beautiful. Thank you."

"You are welcome. I will get my tuning tools then. Wait here."

The Bending Branch

"Yes, thank you."

Taree felt as if she were in a daze. She had so many questions but was almost afraid to ask them. She thought it was probably best to begin with her dad. She also decided she'd wait to mention the piano and instead make a copy of Matt's picture of the mysterious woman as the method to broach the subject.

The Bending Branch

Chapter 26

That night, after Mrs. Akiyama had left, along with the moving men, Taree sat at her piano and played. It had such a rich and vibrant sound. She made a mental note to do as Mr. Akiyama had suggested and take his appraisal to her insurance company to have her rental insurance raised to cover it.

When the door bell rang, she went to the door, saw Rinji through the peephole, and let him in. He walked in and immediately crossed to the piano. "So, what do you think?" he asked.

She crossed over to where he was. "It's amazing. Thank you, Rinji."

The Bending Branch

"You are quite welcome," he laughed. "But my parents did all the work. Have you played it yet?"

"Just before you rang the bell," she admitted.

"And?"

"You were right. My old friend is better than ever!"

Rinji smiled. "I love you, Taree. I'm glad you are happy."

"Me too," she laughed. "I even have a plan to try to covertly question my dad."

"How?"

"I plan to use Matt's drawing and mention my memories and dreams."

"That might work," Rinji agreed. "Do you think it will upset him?"

"Less likely to upset him than mom, I would think. Besides, he's always been more involved in my life than she has and I've always wondered why. I'm thinking he's probably the one with the answers even though it is probably mom's mother."

"When are you going to move in your stuff? I could sure go for a movie, or even a chair to sit in."

Taree walked back to where he stood. "We have the stairs."

"Or my couch and television."

"Yeah, we could go to your place if you'd like."

"You seem to be doing well with all that has happened today."

"I'll bet you thought you'd find me in a puddle on the floor, right?"

"The thought had crossed my mind. What gives?"

"I have you for always," Taree chimed.

The Bending Branch

"And here I thought I was going to get lectured for hiding my affection from my parents."

"No, I understood. It would have been disrespectful."

"She's growing up before my very eyes," he teased.

"Yes, I am," she agreed. She reached up and kissed him on the cheek.

"You realize it will always be disrespectful, right?"

"So long as we have time alone, simple affection in public is fine," she reasoned.

"Glad you are being so practical," he chuckled.

"I'll have to face my dad on my own, though. I'm not looking forward to that."

"And don't you start work on Monday?"

"Yeah, that's why I'd like to get the story before then."

"Well, unfortunately I should head home. Unlike you, I've got to work tomorrow."

"I'll miss you," she pouted.

"I know."

"Don't I at least get a good night hug?"

Rinji wrapped her into his muscular arms. "Not a kiss?" he suggested.

"I thought you'd never ask," she agreed.

"I have to ask?" he groaned.

Taree laughed. "No." And, as she planted a quick kiss on his lips, he hugged her more tightly and kissed her again. When he moved away, she tightened her grip. "Never ask," she whispered. "Just kiss."

Rinji grinned. "You need to let go so I can leave."

The Bending Branch

Taree sighed. "Good night, Rinji." Then she let her arms drop to her side.

"Good night, Taree," he returned, as he moved on out through the door.

Chapter 27

The next day, Taree called Narissa. She asked her if she'd been serious when she said that she didn't need to hire movers for the storage unit. Narissa reminded her that two of her brothers owned a moving company. She gave Taree the number.

Within three hours, Taree's townhome was filled with furniture and boxes. The brothers would only allow her to pay for the mileage and gas. She thanked them again and then they left.

After unpacking and setting up the computer, Taree took out the printer, copier, and scanner and made a copy of the picture that Matt had drawn. She then phoned her dad and asked if she and he could have lunch.

The Bending Branch

She told him that she really wanted to talk about something. He agreed and she left the house to meet him.

Once they had placed their orders, Taree cautiously introduced her subject. "Dad, I don't want you to become angry and I want you to know that I trust that you have always done everything you did with my best interests in mind, but I wanted to ask you something that has been bewildering to me throughout the years."

"Okay, Taree. I'll try to be objective then."

"As far back as I can remember, I've had both memories and dreams about an unknown woman. She is always smiling down at me. I was very young at the time and I do not know who she is. I suspect that she may have been my grandmother. I have a drawing that someone drew for me, based on

The Bending Branch

my description, and I'd like to ask you if you could please tell me who she is."

Her dad quietly took the picture. The surprise in his eyes revealed that the picture was as accurate as Taree knew it to be. "Taree, I am sorry that you've had this unexplained memory. Your mother thought it best to never mention her parents because you were so young when we came to America. She believed that you would not remember. This is your grandmother, Kazue. Your grandmother was half German and half Japanese. She was a beautiful lady."

He cleared his throat. "Your great-grandfather, your grandmother's dad, was a German living in Japan. He married a young Japanese girl and they lived, happily, in Japan, until something happened and his wife died. Filled with grief, your grandmother's dad

The Bending Branch

moved, with her, to somewhere in the Soviet Union. It is unclear as to why he moved them there, but this is where your grandmother met your grandfather. He, too, was a German living in the Soviet Union. When your grandfather died, she had nowhere to turn. His parents refused to accept that their son had married a woman who was not full German."

Taree's father continued. "But your grandmother was a very special friend to my mother. My parents insisted that she, and her daughter, come to live with us. She became my family's live-in housekeeper. We all were residents of a remote area of the Soviet Union at the time. When your mother turned eighteen, a man of wealth, great power, and much influence, tried to force your grandmother to give your mother, to him, as

The Bending Branch

a wife. I was the oldest boy in our family and your mother and I had grown up, together, as good friends. I agreed to marry her so that this man could not have her. Everyone in the town knew that this man did not treat women the way he should, but no one had ever dared to defy him."

He paused, again, as the waitress returned with their drinks. When she moved away, he carried on. "This next part might be hard for you to hear, but you will need to listen in order to understand. My family began to face persecution because of this marriage, but we managed to do okay. My parents sent my younger brother to live with an uncle in Germany; he was my mother's uncle. My brother eventually took this uncle's last name. It was the only protection he had. My brother's family is the one that you visited

The Bending Branch

and stayed with while in Germany. Anyhow, my parents were angry with me. Although they agreed with what I had done, they said I was wrong to have expected to live under their roof. I had brought persecution to our home."

He stopped again as the waitress brought the food. "Soon, your mother became pregnant. You were born into our family and given my last name. But our last name had become a curse; the spited tycoon had seen to this. Your grandmother blamed herself for this persecution even though I was the one who had taken it upon myself to save her daughter; she began to search for family in Japan and was found by a distant relative. This relative came to the Soviet Union and paid for my family, your mom, and me to leave to America. Your grandmother, a

The Bending Branch

talented pianist, sent her piano with you; she spent the night engraving it with her love. She watched us leave on a ship for America and then she left the Soviet Union to go live with her Japanese relatives."

Taking a drink, he paused, watching his daughter's face. "I never knew why we were Germans living in the Soviet Union, but I was excited to be moving to America. Your mother, though, did not want to move to America and she was so angry at your grandmother. She would not forgive her for having married such a weak husband and for not demanding that his German family accept and support them. She had the piano painted gold because we wouldn't let her sell it: my mother took if from her and told her that it belonged to her granddaughter. The piano had been a wedding gift from your

The Bending Branch

grandfather's grandparents and he at least had the sense to engrave it with your grandmother's picture so that it could not be taken from her if he died. He had thought she would sell it so that she, along with their daughter, would be able to leave the country. But you grandmother could not bear to part with it. She loved that piano. Later—once we finally had a house large enough—my mother moved the piano into your room."

Her father paused to eat. Taree had tears in her eyes. "Father, why do I have a Japanese name? If mother was so angry at grandmother, why would she name me Taree?"

"I named you Taree," he admitted. "And it sealed my fate. I, too, became her enemy. Your mother was very sick when she had you. The nurses believed that the tycoon had paid

The Bending Branch

someone in order to make her sick. She almost died. The doctor said that you were strong, like a branch that bends but does not break. He said you came early, but you were healthy. Your grandmother, Kazue, told me that Taree meant bending branch. So I named you Taree. At times your mother tells me that if I was going to betray her anyway, then it would have been best, for everyone, if I had left her to marry the aged tycoon. My answer is always the same: it would not have been best for you, Taree, and you are worth all the sacrifices that we have ever made. And it would not have been best for her, no matter how much she might insist it would have been. Even though I know she does not mean what she says, we were never in love. It was a marriage of convenience."

The Bending Branch

"And she has always blamed me for her inability to have more children. I understand now. Did she leave you, father, or was this separation mutual?"

"She left me for her law partner. They are going to start their own law office together. I am glad that she is finally finding happiness. I'm not so thrilled that she says she has paid her dues and will no longer sacrifice herself to me. She makes me sound like an ogre."

"I knew she seemed disinterested in me, but I always thought she wasn't well. I am sorry, Dad."

"I like to believe that she isn't well, Taree. That the sickness changed her."

"Is it a problem that I am dating a Japanese man? Will mom disown me like she did her parents?"

The Bending Branch

"I don't know. In my own way, I do love your mother. I don't believe I could live with a person for as long as I lived with her and not form some sort of bond. But she is a harsh woman. You might have to choose. All I can say is to choose wisely."

"Why couldn't you get me at the airport, then? I heard a young female giggling in the background. I thought you were the one who had left mom."

Her dad began to laugh. "Oh, no, nothing like that. Our office was having a party for our clients and I was the one who had to give the presentation. Also, it was my responsibility to get people safely into cabs so they'd make it back to their hotels if they had too much to drink. I hated to tell you 'No' but I was the only one who was prepared to give the power point. And this particular

The Bending Branch

client brings in a lot of revenue." He really started to have a chuckle. "Imagine, your old, proper, dad . . ." He couldn't even bring himself to finish his sentence.

Taree started to laugh, too. "I thought it seemed out of character, but . . . well, thank you for your honesty, Dad. Will mom be angry if I restore my piano?"

"Probably, but she has no right. It's your piano. And it was a glorious sight before she painted it gold. I think you *should* restore it. Your mother's mom left you a message in Japanese. You have the right to know what she said."

"Is grandma still alive?" she wondered aloud.

"No, I'm sorry. I attended her funeral when you were in Kindergarten, I think."

The Bending Branch

"I think I remember that. Mom refused to go. Well, that's okay. Grandma lives in my memories," Taree reassured.

For the first time in years, Taree and her dad hugged when they parted. She was sad for her mom and the bitterness that had been allowed to take root. But she was happy that she now knew the whole story. She took out her phone and called Rinji, hoping that he might be taking his lunch break. When she got his voice mail, she decided to leave a message. "Does it matter that I'm only one-eighth Japanese and seven-eighths German?" She knew, to him, it didn't, but she said it anyway, giggling as she hung up the phone.

The Bending Branch

Chapter 28

Taree went shopping so she could fill her fridge. She decided that she would cook for Rinji that night, if he could come with such short notice. She loved to cook and bake and was looking forward to showcasing this talent. After all, it seems to have always been said that *the way to a man's heart is through his stomach*. And even though she already appeared to have his heart, Taree figured it could only add to his appreciation for her.

Again, he did not answer his phone. She left another message. "I'm planning a wonderful dinner for tonight, if you can come. Please let me know as soon as you can so that I don't do all of this work for nothing." Then she began preparations for Steak Au

The Bending Branch

Poivre, Scalloped Cheese Potatoes, Vegetarian Cabbage Rolls, and homemade bread. She decided to serve fruit for dessert and water as their drink. About two hours into her preparations, her doorbell rang. She assumed it would be Rinji, but checked the peephole anyhow. It was Narissa.

Narissa's face was soaked with tears and her makeup was running down her neck. This did not stop Taree from hugging her, though. After calming her down, she learned that Narissa's brothers had seen her boyfriend out with another woman. Since she and he had been exclusive for the last three years, Narissa had given him the benefit of the doubt and had gone to discuss who this woman might have been. Her brothers had tried to warn her that they'd seen them *kissing*, but she had dismissed their warnings,

The Bending Branch

not wanting to believe that they were *those* kind of kisses . . . like her brothers couldn't tell what kind of kisses they were. When he didn't answer the door, she used her key and went in. She had caught them in bed together, had called her brothers to find out where Taree lived, and had come straight here.

Taree hugged her again and then asked her if she could sit at the kitchen table so that Taree could continue to work on the dinner. Narissa instead agreed to help with the meal, since it would take her mind off things, and they could still talk while not falling behind on the schedule that Taree had set. Narissa left to wash up in the bathroom. In the time that it took for Narissa to return, everything was already in the oven or on the stove, cooking. Only the fruit needed to be cleaned and chopped.

The Bending Branch

Rinji still had not called. Taree was beginning to think that he wasn't coming. Had she offended him with her silly message? She tried not to think about it and concentrated on Narissa and the fruit.

When everything was ready, Taree refrigerated what needed to be kept cold and lowered the heating temperatures for what needed to be kept warm. Narissa thanked her for her time and attention and promised to call later. She had to go to work.

Finally, after another half an hour had passed by, Rinji called. "Am I too late?" he asked.

"No, I've been keeping everything warm," she admitted.

"I'm sorry. I didn't get your messages until just now. I had to work late because Julia

The Bending Branch

went into premature labor. I accidentally left my phone home today."

"That's okay. I had a friend in crisis as well. So it all worked out. Just come as soon as you can."

Once they had finished eating the meal, Taree asked if he wanted dessert now, or later. He opted for later, so they cleaned the table and then moved to the living room to watch some television. "I see you finally moved in," he commented.

"Wow, yeah, that was this morning. It has really been a long day."

"So what was the crisis?"

Taree told him about Matt's sister and what had happened. He seemed sympathetic but pointed out that they had been talking about moving in together just the week before. He felt badly, but suggested the guy

The Bending Branch

got cold feet. "It doesn't have to be wedding jitters, these days," he said. "Maybe he panicked when he saw they were taking it to the next level."

"Probably. She's such a good person, too."

"Oh, did you talk to your dad today? Is that what the heritage message meant?"

"Yes, I did." She went on to explain the story to Rinji as her dad had related it to her. She left out the possible problem that her mother might have with the Japanese and she didn't mention the question that she had asked her father about him, either. There was no reason to; she would never even consider walking away, regardless of her mother's feelings or threats.

After two shows had run, Rinji asked, "So how about that dessert?"

The Bending Branch

Taree went to the kitchen and brought back the fruit. Rinji laughed: "Oh, I see. You really meant dessert."

"Rinji!" she exclaimed, blushing. Then she sat down next to him and began to laugh, as well. "Actually, that would have been a good idea. Kisses would have saved me quite a bit of preparation."

He set his fruit on the coffee table and then took hers and did the same. "I think I'll have both," he decided. He kissed her on the forehead, first, and then moved his lips along her cheeks. When his lips finally touched hers, she readily responded. As they kissed, he gently pushed her back against the couch cushions and she did her best to keep him near. Whenever he would move away, she'd pull herself back to him. When he shifted to the side, she at last laid her head on his

The Bending Branch

shoulder, pressing her nose into his neck. "Mmm," she said in contentment. "I love the way you smell and taste."

Rinji hugged her closer. He was about to say something when his phone interrupted. "Hello?" he answered. He slid Taree to the side and sat up. After about five minutes, he hung up. "Julia had a boy," he shared. "Mother and son are both doing well."

Taree smiled. "I'm glad," she responded. "Were you going to say something before your phone rang?" she asked.

Rinji pondered and then said, "I think I was, but I don't remember. Sorry."

"It's okay." She picked up her fruit and began to eat it. Rinji did the same. Taree's cell phone rang. After a short conversation she hung up. "Narissa, thanking me for today," she explained.

The Bending Branch

When the fruit was finished, Taree took the dishes into the kitchen. Rinji came up behind her as she rinsed them in the sink. "Can I stay here with you tonight?" he surprisingly asked. You still have the airbed in addition to yours, right?"

Taree assured him that she did and tried not to question his reason. He gave her an answer, anyhow. "I moved my stuff to my new house today but it's presently all in the garage. I wanted to clean before I move stuff into the house so the carpets are all wet, etc."

"You got your house! Congratulations!" she squealed. "I'm so happy for you."

Rinji laughed. "I can tell. So can I stay here?"

"Of course you can. I owe you at least one stay over," she teased.

The Bending Branch

"Not more? I can never ask again?" Rinji played along.

"Oh, you can always ask," she said, nonchalantly.

"And you'll always say yes," he asserted.

"Yes, Rinji, I will always say yes," she agreed, obediently, with a gleam in her eyes. "I am so glad that you came tonight. And I am glad that you trust me enough to stay."

Rinji smiled. "And you, of course, trust me."

They went back into the living room. "Do you mind if I play a bit on my piano?" she asked.

"I would love to hear you play," he consented. And when she had finished, he had fallen asleep on the couch. Taree covered him with an afghan and then went on up the stairs to sleep.

The Bending Branch

Chapter 29

The alarm went off at four in the morning to remind her to wake up Rinji. She crawled out of bed, visited the bathroom, washed her face and brushed her teeth, and then headed down the stairs. Rinji was already awake, sitting up on the edge of the couch. "What are you doing up?" he queried.

"Just wanted to be sure that you didn't miss work; that's all," she yawned.

"Come sit with me a second, will you?" he asked.

Taree had stopped halfway down the stairs. She continued on down and then sat next to him. He remained quiet. Then he suddenly took her hand in his. "Are you happy?" he questioned.

The Bending Branch

She carefully contemplated her answer before she spoke. "Most of the time, I think, but to be honest, not always. Why?"

"Do you expect me to make you happy? How do you see me?"

"People have to choose happiness, Rinji. And sometimes people have to set aside their fantasies to realize that they are happy. No one is happy all the time. I'm content, though. You add depth to my life. If you cause me pain, it's not going to make me happy, but I'll probably learn something from it. If you have a burden, I want to share it with you. I don't really expect you to make me happy, but I enjoy being with you . . . even if being with you means sharing a few tears."

"But how do you see me?" he repeated.

"You're my best friend. We can be sad together, happy together, angry together,

The Bending Branch

quiet together, and we still remain friends throughout it all. We've had good days and bad days and I wouldn't change any of them."

"And moving into the romantic realm hasn't changed any of this?"

"Of course it has. I feel things more deeply and I also find myself turning to get your opinion or advice as if you are right next to me and then realizing how it seems a part of me stays with you even when we are apart. Sometimes I ache to be near you. But I have come to understand that it all exists because I know you so well and we are such good friends. I trust you."

"I feel the same way. Sometimes it hurts to be away from you. Yet I never really feel alone . . . not even when I get the voice mail when I try to call."

The Bending Branch

"And this bothers you?" She could tell that it did and she suddenly felt almost as if the very thought had pierced through her heart and left her breathless. She had walked beyond this irrational fear—the fear of loss if something should happen to him. She had already come to the conclusion that having even one day more with him was worth any number of days in which he might no longer exist. It was not the fear that he would leave her intentionally; it was the fear of losing him to fate. She realized that this must be what he was now going through while thinking of her.

"I refuse to be dependant," he stated. She had also already faced this fear. She had grasped that she was not truly dependant, although life without Rinji would not be as full. She would continue to live on and learn to live and love again if she had to. But she was intent on spending every second of life that she could with him. It seemed that, despite his careful planning, he was behind her on recognizing and sorting things out. And she knew that she could not help him. He had to find his way by himself.

When she didn't answer him, he turned to look her in the eyes. "I think I need to take some space," he told her. He expected her to cry, to beg. Instead, she surprised him.

"Rinji, you take whatever time and space that you need. I trust you to come back to me. And if you can't, then I'll accept that and deal with it when I have to." She kissed him on the cheek. "I love you. Do what you have to so you can find your way to being content. I'll be waiting for you to either return or to say good-bye. Just don't make me wait for your answer forever."

The Bending Branch

"You're not angry?" He had expected her to behave immaturely. This would have been so much easier if she had given him reason to doubt his love for her.

"No. I love you. I want you to be content. But please remember that being content and being happy is not the same thing." She kissed him again on the cheek. "Good-bye, Rinji," she whispered. "You know where to find me when you sort things out." And Taree left him on the couch, reminding him that he had work to go to as she climbed the stairs back up to her room. She let out a sigh as she heard him close the door.

The Bending Branch

Chapter 30

Three months had passed since that morning on the couch. Taree had begun to keep a journal of things she wished she could have discussed or shared with him. She would write out her thoughts or ideas and then quietly reclose her designated book.

She kept the book in her purse and she never wrote in any names, just in case it was ever stolen. But writing would help her to sort through the many incidences, or events, without allowing her to feel alone. She was growing steadily stronger.

She truly enjoyed her job and she also took pleasure in the benefits that come with a six-figure salary. Her wardrobe, along with stylish makeup and hair, brought confidence

The Bending Branch

to all the clients that she worked with. The company was talking about promoting her and giving her a raise, although they also considered the hole that she would leave if they did this. It made Taree smile.

Yet today, she could not help that she carried a twinge of loneliness. Today her mother was getting remarried. Rather than receiving an invitation or a request that Taree be a maid of honor, she instead had received what might be considered a rejection. Her mother had gone to the trouble of sending both she, and her dad, what looked like an invitation but instead carried words of hate.

The rejection had basically stated that her mom had divorced them both and that she was starting a new life without them. She wanted nothing to do with either of them, nor

The Bending Branch

with any relatives that came with them, either past, present, or future.

Taree decided not to put this entry into her journal. She kept the written rejection, however, since it was legally signed by her mother and might prove useful some day.

As she pondered how close she and her father had become, Taree called him to be sure that he was okay. He assured her that he was not alone and that he had gone to visit his parents so she need not worry.

It was a breezy, but warm Saturday. Seldom did she go on walks. She remembered, too often, how close Rinji's house was and she did not want to run into him. She was contemplating, however, that maybe she should when the door bell rang.

The peephole revealed Narissa, two of her older brothers, and their mom. Opening the

The Bending Branch

door, she was sure that her face was the definition of inquisitive. It turned out that they had read about her mom's wedding, had called Taree's dad, and had decided to take her along with them on a family outing. She readily agreed to the distraction.

Matt's brothers flirted with her while Narissa argued that they should leave her alone. No one knew that Taree and Rinji had called it quits and Taree wanted it this way. As she came back from a swim with Narissa, she suddenly felt a familiar set of eyes lock onto her. She looked up in confusion. Sure enough, it was Rinji. Her smile slid from her face as she noticed a petite Japanese woman at his side. Before Narissa could notice, Taree had directed her in a different path and had pasted the smile back onto her face.

The Bending Branch

The rest of the picnic was a blur. After about an hour, Taree realized that she had a sun-inflicted headache and asked to be taken home. Narissa obliged, telling her family that she'd return shortly.

Once home, Taree showered and then took some aspirin. She also took some allergy medication to help her sleep. Her headache had evolved into a nauseating migraine.

By Monday, she began to feel as if she had the flu. She took her temperature and the thermometer read 102.3 degrees Fahrenheit. She called her dad to see if she could stay with him. Instead, he came to stay with her.

When her fever rose, and she began to vomit, Taree's dad drove her to the hospital. The symptoms reminded him of his wife when Taree had been born; they had suspected poisoning. He wisely kept this information to himself.

After much testing, it was determined that Taree had sun poisoning and was also dehydrated. She would have to stay in the hospital. She asked her dad to please be sure that her employers knew. She couldn't remember if she had called them. He promised to take care of it.

As she fell in and out of consciousness, Taree began to doubt the reality around her. She could not tell where dreams began and ended and what was real or fiction. She finally asked the nurse not to let anyone in other than her dad. She explained it was too confusing and exhausting for her to follow. The nurse obliged.

Finally, Taree was released. She went home, took care of all the bills, and then

The Bending Branch

showered in her own shower. She was so happy to again be in her own bed.

The Bending Branch

Chapter 31

The next morning brought a new weekend. Taree awoke to the memory of having seen Rinji at the beach. Tears fell down her cheeks as she began to pack away his memories with those belonging to Matt. Once everything had been boxed, she poured herself into the piano. Her playing was filled with the anguish that she had grown accustomed to in her past.

When the door bell rang, she ignored it. She just continued to play song after song. Finally, she returned to her room and collapsed on the bed in exhaustion.

Later that day, she awoke to what sounded like knocking. She went back downstairs and peered out through the peephole. No one

The Bending Branch

appeared to be there, so she opened the door. A note fell to her feet, so she picked it up and went back inside.

She dropped the note on the kitchen counter and then went to her computer and caught up on some work. Her inbox was filled with notes from both clients and friends, all wishing her well. She placed these into a folder for the moment so she could answer what appeared to be more important.

It then occurred to her that she was hungry, so she went back to the kitchen to get a snack. She remembered the note. Opening it, she could tell immediately that it was from Rinji. She was about to drop it onto the counter again, when she realized that she could not: she had to know.

Taree, I miss you beyond belief. I came by after I saw you at the beach—to explain—but

The Bending Branch

it appears you are avoiding me. No matter what part of the day that I ring your bell, you do not answer. I tried to call, but the number sends me to voicemail that is full. What good does it do me to know where to find you if you are shutting me out? You said you would be waiting for me. I can only continue to hope. I trust you. Rinji.

Taree went back to the door and opened it. She stepped out onto the porch. As she turned to go back inside, she instinctively twisted so she could look out once more. Rinji was running toward her. She moved back onto the porch and waited.

When he reached her side, his arms immediately encased her. She, however, remained unresponsive. He realized that this was going to take some work. "Can we please

The Bending Branch

go inside?" he pleaded. "Will you allow me to explain? Can we talk?"

She did not answer but instead turned, indicating that he should follow. He scanned her face from the side. The glow in her eyes was missing and she'd lost some weight. But she had looked fine on the beach, less than two weeks before.

She went into the kitchen and fixed herself a sandwich. She offered him the same, but he declined. Then she poured herself a glass of milk and carried it all to the coffee table in the living room. "I apologize for not answering the door," she offered in a methodical tone. "I contracted sun poisoning when I went to the beach and was hospitalized; it's been less than twenty-four hours since I returned home."

The Bending Branch

Rinji seemed relieved, yet concerned. "But you are all right now?" he asked, politely.

"Well, they did let me leave," she reasoned, "so I would hope so."

He then noticed the packed boxes in the corner. "You're moving again?"

"Well, the purpose for choosing this location seemed to have run its course and, since I was trying not to run into you, I've not had the freedom to go on walks, or use the park. It's kind of ironic that I ran into you across town, instead," she explained.

"I never asked you to intentionally avoid me, Taree. I only asked for some space."

"I know," she agreed. "But this was your space before it was mine. So, I've decided to look for something new again."

He shocked her with his next words, "Move in with me."

The Bending Branch

"Why would you say that?" she argued. "So much has happened since you left that morning. I don't even know where to begin."

"Am I to assume that you didn't mean it when you told me to take whatever time and space I needed and that you trusted me to come back?"

"I did mean it. I meant it with every fiber of my existence."

"But you doubt me?"

"No, Rinji, I doubt myself. Something happened that really hurt me. I am still working it out and it has the potential to change me. I am fighting that change."

"You're not talking about the beach, are you?" he perceived.

"No, I'm not. Your eyes told me all I needed to know. Once I recovered from seeing you

The Bending Branch

and having you so close to me, I saw the answer in your eyes. You still love me."

"Yes, Taree, I do. So why have you hidden all traces of me?"

"I was so happy to know that you still love me. Then I recalled that I'm not that same person, and..."

Rinji interrupted. "Do you still love me?"

Taree couldn't lie. "Yes."

"Then share your pain with me." Rinji was different. He had become stronger and determined.

Taree crossed to the box where she had carefully placed her memories of both Matt and Rinji. She pulled out the topmost envelope and handed it to him.

He then opened it and began to silently read: *Ms. Ava Becker requests the absence of your presence at her upcoming marriage and from the remainder of her life. She has divorced and no longer accepts the name of Schulz, or anyone or anything associated with such name. Any life that was led while using the name of Ava Schulz is hereby considered eradicated as if it had never taken place.* Ms. Ava Becker, obviously Taree's mom, had even taken the time to personally sign her own signature, just to be clear.

Rinji had tears in his eyes when he finished reading. Taree had never seen him come even close to having shed a tear. Yet here he sat, eyes brimming. He set the offending cardboard onto the coffee table.

"Come," he insisted. He took her hand and brought her over to the piano. He lifted the lid to reveal the message from her grandmother. Do you remember what it

The Bending Branch

says? Taree shook her head, trying hard not to allow her tears to join his.

First he read it to her in Japanese. It sounded so musical. She had always delighted in the way he spoke her name, but when he spoke Japanese, she melted. Then he translated it, just as his father had done: "To my beautiful granddaughter, Taree. I send my piano in my place. Live well in America. Remember that I love you, Kazue."

"Taree," he reminded, "Your father loves you, your father's parents love you, Matt loved you, Matt's family loves you, your German relatives love you, and your Grandma Kazue loved you. Most importantly, though, *I* love you." Rinji drew Taree into his arms and brought her as close to himself as he possibly could. "*I* love you," he repeated. Then he gently kissed her forehead, her eyes,

The Bending Branch

and her cheeks. In conclusion, he kissed her lips.

Taree returned kiss for kiss and when he raised his head to scan her face, she drew him back to her and kissed him again. "Thank you, Rinji," she murmured. "Thank you for reminding me who I am."

"So," he prompted, "are you going to move in with me?"

"What are your intentions, Sir?" she teased.

"I thought my objective was clear, Miss Schulz. I want you to become Akiyama Taree."

Taree was again filled with joy. "I love you," she said, simply. "It's all I will ever want to be."

Made in the USA
Middletown, DE
23 July 2017